Breaking the BIKER

CASSIE ALEXANDRA

PROLOGUE

RAINA

Breaking
BIKE

"I**S THAT HIM?**"

Cole smashed his cigarette out in the ashtray of the van.

"Yeah."

I stared at the gray-haired man in the Gold Viper's cut, hating him with every fiber of my being. He was getting onto his chopper behind Griffin's, the strip-joint he apparently owned. "Don't you dare fucking lose him."

He frowned. "Relax, Raina. I'm not going to lose him."

I pulled the revolver out of the glove-compartment and checked the chamber, making sure it was still loaded. It was supposed to be untraceable. Early this morning, my brother, Cole, had given it to me, although not so willingly, and I wanted to make sure that he hadn't removed the bullets. He thought I was making a mistake, and hell… maybe I was. But I didn't care. Now that my baby boy was gone, all I wanted was to destroy the man responsible for his death. Slammer, the club president of the Gold Vipers. He'd ordered the drive-by that had killed my two-year-old son and there was no way in hell I was going to let him live to gloat about it.

"I still think you should let the club handle this," repeated Cole as we followed Slammer's motorcycle out of the parking lot at a safe distance. "Killing him without their approval isn't going to get me patched anytime soon."

I stared at him in disbelief.

Billy was dead and he was worried about getting patched?

"Do you honestly think that I care about pissing off your club? As far as I'm concerned, both the Gold Vipers and the Devil's Rangers can

1

burn in hell. That also goes for your dumbass girlfriend, Patty."

Cole didn't say anything. I knew that in his own way, he was struggling with the fact that his nephew was dead, too. He'd loved Billy and had even admitted to feeling partly responsible. Cole was currently a prospect for the Devil's Rangers, and it had been his girlfriend who'd shown up with my son, uninvited, to a club bash, when she was supposed to be giving him a bath and tucking him into bed. Instead, she'd dragged him to the party just to check up on Cole and make sure he wasn't cheating. Her jealous insecurities had contributed to my son's death, as well as to her own injuries, since she'd taken a bullet to the shoulder. But unlike my two-year-old son, fate had shown mercy on her that day. Now it was taking everything I had not to revoke that decision and kill the stupid bitch myself.

"So what, you want to kill Patty, too?"

"It's certainly been running through my mind," I muttered angrily. "I really can't believe you'd get involved with someone so fucking dense. And what in the hell was I thinking by *allowing* her to watch him?"

"I know. She's a head-case."

"Obviously."

"It's over between us."

"I hope so, because if I ever see her again, I'll kick her ass all the way back to the hospital."

"I wouldn't blame you," he said, flicking his cigarette ash.

I went on. "She had no right bringing Billy to any party. If she would have stayed at my place, like I was paying her to do," my voice broke, "my baby would be alive right now."

His eyes softened. "I know. It was a fucked up move; I'm sure she'll regret it for the rest of her life."

It was too early for me to feel sorry for anyone else. Especially Patty. She was twenty-two. She knew better than to bring a child to a beer bash, no matter what the reason was. "Good. Maybe it will save someone else's life."

"Maybe." Cole let out a ragged sigh. "Look, I know everything seems hopeless right now, but I want you to remember that you're not alone, Raina. You still have me," he said, reaching over to squeeze my hand. "And Uncle Sal. Don't you ever forget that."

Nodding, I looked out the passenger window, to try and pull myself together. At that moment, all I really wanted to do was lie in Billy's bed, and curl up with his pillow, which still smelled like him. I wanted to imagine that I was holding him in my arms as he stared up at me with those big brown eyes.

I wuv you, mommy...

My chest tightened and I closed my eyes, forcing the tears away. Now was not the time to lose my shit. Cole would surely pull over and Slammer would ride off.

"For the record, I still think this is a very bad idea," he said, pushing in the dashboard lighter.

"I never said it was a good one. Just that it needed to happen," I replied bitterly.

Cole had tried talking me out of it so many times. Finally, I told him that I'd do it without his help and that had worried him even more. As much as he loved me, Cole was chauvinistic and believed that women couldn't handle anything on their own without making a mistake. Especially if it was crime-related. Being a prospect for the Devil's Rangers, I was pretty confident that he'd already been involved in some of their illegal dealings and thought himself to be an expert. Another reason to hate my brother's MC as well as their enemies. They were turning him into a criminal.

"Do you really think Mark would want you risking your life like this?"

Mark had been Billy's father. He'd died the year before in a car accident. He'd been working eighteen-hour days, trying to earn extra income so that we could buy a house. It was believed that he'd nodded off on his way home on the morning of the accident. His Jeep had drifted over the center line of a busy freeway, hitting a tree head-on. It was said that Mark's death had been quick and that he hadn't felt a thing. Billy had been shot in the shoulder, which I knew had to have been painful. Unfortunately, he'd died before I'd made it to the hospital. I hadn't even been able to comfort him.

"I don't want to hear it anymore," I said, wiping the moisture from under my eyes. "Slammer is going to get what's coming to him, so just keep following the asshole and stop badgering me about it."

Cole lit another cigarette and became quiet.

We followed Slammer for a few more blocks until he parked his bike in the parking lot of a local credit union. It was shortly after six and the place appeared to be closed.

"What's he doing?" I asked, sitting up straighter.

Cole frowned. "I don't know. Maybe he's withdrawing some money from the ATM? Looks like you have to go inside to use the machine."

"Hmm," I said, biting my lower lip.

He parked the van on the side of the street across from the bank. We watched as Slammer got off of his bike and walked over to the door with the flashing ATM sign.

"See, I told you," said my brother, smirking. "He's probably making a withdrawal. Should rob the fucker, too."

"I'm not after his dirty money," I said, shoving the gun into my sweatshirt. I pulled the hood over my dark hair and slipped on a pair of sunglasses. "After I go into the building, pull up to the doorway. This shouldn't take too long."

"Jesus, you're really going through with this?" he asked, staring at me like I was some kind of alien.

"This was never meant to be a game, little brother," I said, opening the door. I got out and hurried across the street, my heart pumping madly in my chest. As I reached the doorway, two women, speed-walking, rounded the corner of the building.

Shit.

They both stepped around me; one looked back over her shoulder with a curious look on her face. I couldn't exactly blame her for being nosy. I was wearing a hoodie, in the middle of summer, and a dark pair of sunglasses. I probably looked like a street punk up to no good.

Not exactly worried about them, I entered the building and was prepared to shoot anyone who got in my way. I had more than one bullet, and part of me toyed with the idea of ending my own miserable life.

When I saw the man responsible for Billy's death alone at the

5

cash machine, I immediately got behind him and pulled the gun out of my pocket.

"I'm almost done here," he mumbled, pushing some buttons.

Staring at the patch of the gold snake on the back of his cut, I cocked the gun and pointed it at him. My hand shook as I tried to hold it straight.

Hearing the click, Slammer's shoulders stiffened up. He turned his head and looked at me. "What in the hell is this? A robbery?"

"You... you're the one who robbed me," I replied, my voice breaking as I pictured my baby's smile and the soft curls that framed his face. I would never again get to kiss those dimpled cheeks or watch him sleep at night.

He'd had the longest eyelashes.

"And now," I glared at him. "You're going to pay, motherfucker."

His face turned white. "Raina?"

I wuv you mommy...

Sobbing, I fired the gun.

ONE

TANK

I HEARD THE JUDGE'S motorcycle pull up to the house and grabbed the bottle of Jack from the counter. There were some things I wanted to discuss with him about the Devil's Rangers, and knew it might be my only chance to talk to him face-to-face for a while. When I stepped outside and noticed that he had his arms around Jessica, I decided to wait. They obviously wanted some privacy and I wasn't thinking clearly anyway. In fact, I was pretty fucking hammered.

Waving at them, I lit a cigarette and sat down on the porch, still trying to wrap my mind around the fact that my old man was really dead and that some stupid bitch, with ties to the Devil's Rangers, had taken him out. That shit was eating me up inside, especially not knowing who the chick was or where in the hell she was hiding out. All I could think about was finding this girl and avenging Slammer's death. But, Raptor was urging me not to take matters into my own hands and to wait until we had all the facts. He'd also convinced me to put it on the table, for a club vote.

"*This has to be done right,*" *he'd said, after the funeral.* "*No more secrets from the rest of the club. Look at what happened with Slammer. We don't exactly know why this girl murdered him in cold blood anyway.*"

"*It doesn't matter. She did it and needs to pay.*"

"*But don't you want to know why?*"

"*I know why. Rumor has it that she's mixed up with the Devil's Rangers. It was more retaliation.*"

"*I don't know. This doesn't feel right. They don't normally send a chick to do a hit. They wouldn't trust her to get the job done.*"

It didn't exactly sound right to me either, but the fact was, my old man was gone and the shooter was going to pay. I didn't care what kind of affiliation she had to the Devil's Rangers or any other club. I needed to punish someone for my old man's death and it was going to be the bitch responsible.

Sighing, I took another drag of my smoke and watched as the Judge drove off and Jessica walked up the steps toward me.

"Hey," she said, smiling sadly.

"Hey."

"Are you okay?"

I nodded.

"If you want to talk…"

"I'm okay," I replied, looking away. Jessica had her own problems to deal with. I wasn't about to stress her out any more than she already was. "I just need some time to myself."

"I understand." She squeezed my shoulder. "Goodnight, Tank."

"Goodnight."

She walked into the house and I finished my cigarette. After tossing the butt into an empty coffee can, I grabbed my cell phone and called Cheeks, one of the club whores. It was getting late, but I was too hopped up on coke to sleep and needed something to take my mind off of shit.

"What's up, Prez?" she asked, sounding pleasantly surprised.

"Hopefully my cock in about thirty minutes or less."

She laughed. "Are you sure you weren't trying to call for a pizza?"

"No, but now that you mention it… can you pick one up on the way over?"

"Seriously?"

I chuckled. "No. Just get your skinny little ass over here. I could use some TLC, darlin'."

"I can do that. Where are you?"

"I'm at Frannie's. Come to think about it, why don't you pick me up and we'll go back to my place? I don't think partying here is a good idea."

"Is that what we're going to do? Party?"

"Yeah, just you and me, Doll. You up for it?"

"Anything for you, Tank. I'll swing by in twenty minutes."

"I'll be waiting," I said and then hung up.

I took another swig from the bottle of Jack and then went into the kitchen, where I wrote a note to Frannie, letting her know where I was headed. Afterward, I went outside and waited for Cheeks. When she picked me up, I lit another cigarette to cover the heavy stench of her perfume. It was some kind of flowery scent that I couldn't stand, but didn't have the heart to tell her.

"You still smoking?" she asked, opening up her window.

"Yeah. You smoke, don't you?"

"I quit last January. It was my New Year's Resolution."

"Good for you," I replied, meaning it. I'd never tried to quit but knew it was a struggle.

"I'm just surprised you still smoke. You obviously work out hard," she replied, nodding toward my arms.

I smiled wickedly. "Darlin', if you haven't noticed, I do everything hard."

11

She laughed. "Yeah."

I took another drag of my smoke. "Truth is, I don't smoke *that* much. Just when I've been drinking." I chuckled. "Course, I'm always drinking."

"That's funny, but seriously, you should start taking better care of yourself, Tank."

I sighed. Cheeks was in her thirties and pretty hot for an older broad, but I wasn't about to let her, or anyone else, nag me about my health. I lifted weights and usually spent an hour a day on cardio. At least I had before Slammer's death. The last two weeks, I'd been slacking. "I didn't call you over to give me a lecture."

"I'm just trying to look out for you," she said, reaching over to squeeze my knee. "I care, you know?"

"You just need to care about this right now," I said, grabbing her hand and putting it on my crotch. "That's all I need you to worry about, darlin'."

"Looks like someone's missed me." She squeezed my cock. "How do you manage to pack it all in there?"

"It isn't easy. In fact, I need to let him out. So that he can stretch and play."

She chuckled.

I pointed toward a vacant gas station up the road. "Why don't you pull behind there?"

"Are you sure you don't want to wait until we get back to your place? I still have to pick up that pizza I ordered, by the way."

"Forget the pizza. I need your mouth right now."

She grinned. "Your wish is my command. I haven't had me any

Tank for a long time."

"Then drive."

Two minutes later, she was giving me head.

I grabbed the back of her head as she bobbed up and down on my knob. "Fuck. Glad it was just cigarettes you gave up, darlin'. Cause that mouth...." I sucked in my breath. "Was made for sucking."

She smiled up at me, her eyes watery.

My cell phone suddenly went off, startling both of us. "Who the hell is calling me at this fucking hour?" I growled.

Cheeks wiped the side of her mouth. "Could be important?"

"It'd better be." I grabbed my phone and was surprised to find that Bastard, the President of the Mother Charter, was calling me after midnight. I cleared my throat and answered the phone.

"Hey, kid," he said. "Sorry to bother you at this hour. Hope you weren't in the middle of something?"

"No problem at all," I replied, slapping Cheek's hand away from my dick as she began playing with it. "Bastard."

Cheeks gave me a surprised look.

"The reason I'm calling you is that I've found out a little more information on who it was that killed your old man."

I sat up straighter. "Who is it?"

"Now, hold up, son. Before I give you the information, I want to remind you that we don't go killing women. That's not who we are."

I sighed.

"You hear me? If I give you this, I want you to give me your word that you won't kill this girl if you find her."

13

"What am I supposed to do with her, then?" I asked, trying to remain calm. My original plan was to take both her and the guy who ordered the hit out.

"You find out who sent her to do the killing and deal with him."

"She should be dealt with, too. She's the one who put the bullet through his head."

"We don't kill women. Besides, my source says that she's been through some family shit and death would probably only be a relief to her."

"Because of her, I've got my own family shit, now."

"Yeah, I know. I'm sorry for Slammer but I'm telling you, the woman is off limits. You can do what you have to, in order to get names, but do not kill her."

I stared out the window frustrated.

"Hey, you there?"

'Yeah."

"You understand? Don't kill her."

I wasn't about to argue with him about it on the phone. I knew that it was a club rule, but so much shit had changed over the last twenty years that they were getting harder to follow.

"I know you're pissed, but don't you forget – you're the president of your charter and need to make sure that you *and* your club abide by the rules we've set. That includes not murdering women or children."

"I know."

"And another thing," he said, raising his voice. "You need to pull your shit together if you want to stay as active president. I know you're mourning Slammer. I get that. But, you need to quit with the cocaine and any other illegal drugs your taking, son. I've heard talk that this isn't exactly recreational for you right now."

I wondered who'd been talking to him. I couldn't imagine Raptor or Horse ratting me out. "I'll take care of it," I replied, knowing that it was the only acceptable answer. Bastard wasn't anyone to argue with, and as much as I would have loved to tell him to 'fuck off", I knew that I had to keep my shit in check. Not only was he the most respected member of the Gold Vipers, but my old man had drilled it into my head that when Bastard told you to jump, you leaped.

"Good. Now, the van that picked up the girl, right after the shooting, is owned by a guy named Cole Johnson. He's a prospect for the Devil's Rangers."

"So, it *was* retaliation."

"Looks that way, doesn't it? I'm still not sure who the girl is, though. I'm sure if you can get your hands on Cole, you'll find out all you need."

"You got an address for him?"

"No. His club is in Davenport, though. That's what my informant told me. Their clubhouse is located in a warehouse, somewhere downtown. Anyway, I'm sure their president ordered your old man's hit. Probably passed down by that fuck-head, Reaper, before The Judge took him out."

"Probably. Who's in charge of the Davenport charter?" I asked.

"The President is a guy named Schmitty. The V.P. is some douchebag named Ronnie."

15

"Okay. Thanks."

"Bring this to the table tomorrow and tell me how you guys want to handle it."

"Will do."

"And Tank, I meant what I said. Don't be spilling some girl's blood over this. Everything is pointing to retaliation by the Devil's Rangers, and you know goddamn well that someone higher up made the call. Those are the ones you concentrate on."

"I understand."

"Good. Now, get some sleep and let me know what your club decides to do, so I'm prepared for any fallout."

"Will do."

We hung up and Cheeks put her hand back on my knee. "Everything okay?"

"It will be. Do me a favor, darlin'? Drop me off at home and we'll do this another night."

She looked surprised. "Let me get this straight, *you* don't want to have sex?"

"Sorry, Cheeks. I just have a lot of shit to think about."

Like how I was going to punish the girl who murdered Slammer without Bastard finding out. Someone probably ordered the hit, but I needed the person who had looked him in the eye and pulled trigger to pay as well. Women wanted to be treated like men?

Right now, I was all for equality.

I might not blow the bitch's brains out, but she wasn't getting away without paying some kind of penance.

16

TWO

RAINA

I WOKE UP TO the sound of my cell phone ringing and groaned when I saw what time it was. One-forty-five p.m. My shift at the bar had started at one.

"I know," I mumbled into the phone. "I'm on my way."

"You'd better be," said Marie, one of the other bartenders. "I have an appointment at two-thirty that I can't miss."

"Sorry. I'll be there as soon as I can."

"You'd better," she said sharply.

Fuck you, I thought, hanging up the phone.

From experience, I knew that Marie's afternoon appointments usually involved a tanning shop or a nail salon. Everything about the girl was fake, except for her personality. She was a bitch and didn't try to pretend otherwise. Not with other women at least. When it came to men, that was an entirely different story. She flirted so badly that it was embarrassing to watch. Especially since she was married. The truth was, I'd lost count of the many times she'd given some guy a ride home, claiming he was too drunk to do it himself. Apparently, none of them were too inebriated to drive her. I'd found out her dirty little secret one night after closing. Her windows had been steamed up and the car rocking. Although I'd never given her shit about it, she'd seen me walk by. That didn't stop her from being a twat toward me. I wasn't even sure why she disliked me so much.

Sighing, I dragged myself out of bed, wondering why I even bothered anymore. Life seemed so agonizingly pointless, now that Billy was gone. Sleeping was hard and waking up was even harder. To try and get my mind off of things, I'd been putting in extra hours

19

at Sal's, the bar my uncle owned. It was summer and it seemed we were always busy, which helped. But at night, when I was alone in my apartment, my heart broke every time I saw Billy's ashes in my living room. I'd had him cremated after Mark's brother, Phillip, had suggested it. It was strange knowing that all that remained of my baby was what was in that pewter urn. But, it was also somewhat comforting, knowing that part of him was close by.

My cell phone went off again, and this time, I noticed it was Sal.

"I'm on my way," I said quickly.

"Relax and take your time. She's scheduled until three anyway."

So, he knew Marie had balled me out. I grunted. "Really?"

"Yes. I see you're scheduled at one."

"Yeah. I'm sorry. It's my fault. I overslept," I admitted.

"I'm willing to let it slide. You've been putting in a lot of overtime. Just get here before Happy Hour at four."

"Thanks, Uncle Sal."

"Anything for you, kid."

Sal was our mother's older brother and had been looking out for me and Cole ever since she'd died of a heart attack six years ago, when I was eighteen. He was single and lived alone. We were close, but not close enough for me to tell him about Slammer.

"How's your brother been?" he asked. "I haven't seen him around lately."

"Okay, I guess. He doesn't say much about himself. He's been too busy worrying about me."

"Sounds like him. Always was a quiet kid."

I didn't mention that Cole was worried about the fact that I'd committed murder. He was also afraid that Slammer's successor, some hothead Neanderthal, would find out who I was. Apparently, he was his son and the word out on the streets was that he'd turn over mountains to find his father's killer. I almost wished him success so that he could put me out of the misery that was now my life.

"He's still a prospect?" he asked.

"Yes." I wasn't exactly thrilled with the idea but when I'd tried talking him out of it a few months back, he wouldn't listen. He'd argued that they were like a brotherhood and once you were patched, they'd have your back for life. In other words – they'd own him for life. Body and soul.

As much as I'd tried to convince him that he was setting himself up for a short-lived future, my brother claimed that being around the club made him feel alive, which right now, I almost envied. But, I didn't trust any motorcycle club that touted they were one-percenters. Even I knew that meant they took the law into their own hands and more than likely had their hands in a lot of illegal shit. Of course, after killing Slammer, I wasn't about to start pointing any fingers. I could only hope that Cole would pull his head out of his ass sooner than later, and come to his senses. I was definitely worried about my twenty-three-year-old brother, I just didn't have the energy to keep badgering him about it. I had my own issues to deal with.

"Wish one of us could talk some sense into him. He's going to get himself killed."

"Don't say that," I said softly. As much as I agreed, I couldn't handle the thought of another death in the family.

"I know you don't want to hear it, Raina, but those guys are poison."

21

"Yeah, I know and I've razzed him about it myself. Cole is stubborn, though. He won't listen to reason."

"Believe me, I know."

"If it's any consolation, he told me that he'd walk away if they made him do anything he didn't feel comfortable with."

Sal laughed humorlessly. "Sounds like a crock of shit to me. It wouldn't be that simple. You can't just walk away from a club like that. Especially if they believe that Cole knows too much."

"In which he probably already does."

"He's only a prospect, so he might not know much of the illegal shit they're involved with *yet*. If you ask me, he should get out right now, before they patch him."

I sighed. "I know. Maybe I'll try and talk to him again."

"You should. I know you love him with all of your heart, Raina. You don't want to lose him."

No, I didn't. Besides, Sal, he was all I had left. "Cole said he's going to try and stop in tonight. I'll see what I can do."

"Here? At the bar?"

"Yes," I replied. "Good thing Marie is getting off. I'd have to punch her in the face if she started hitting on him again."

"She'd better watch herself," said Sal. "Marie's going to go home with the wrong man one of these days. I keep telling her she should get a divorce."

"You can't talk sense into a woman who thinks she's smarter than everyone else."

"I know. So Cole's coming down, huh?"

"I think so. He's out of town, I guess. But he plans on getting back early this evening."

"I hope he doesn't bring any of those pricks from the club. They're always trying to start things with my regulars."

"No. He wouldn't," I replied. Cole knew how Sal felt about the Devil's Rangers.

"Okay, then. I guess I'd better let you go so you can get your butt down here. Sorry I kept you."

Leave it to Sal for apologizing, when I was the one who'd overslept. "Obviously, it's not a problem I'll be there as soon as I can."

"I know you will."

Knowing that Marie was in a hurry, I took my time in the shower, and for the first time in weeks, applied some makeup to cover up the dark circles under my tired eyes. Noticing they were also bloodshot, I grabbed the bottle of eye-drops and took care of the problem before adding mascara to my lashes. When I was finished getting ready for work, I was a little startled at my reflection. My cheeks were gaunt, and my dark hair looked dull and lifeless. Plus, I was drowning in my clothes. My voluptuous size twelve body was twenty pounds thinner; the weight I'd been prior to my pregnancy and one I'd struggled to get back to. But now, I couldn't care less about my figure. I'd gain it all back and then some just to hold my son one more time.

23

THREE

TANK

AFTER I CALLED the meeting to order the following afternoon we went through our financials and then got down to the discussion of prospects. Because of his reputation with women, we voted in Taylor Adams, A.K.A. "Tail", as a new member, and then brought him into the meeting to present him with his new cut.

"Thanks, Prez, And you guys, too," he said, glancing around the table. "I'm honored and humbled to be admitted into your club. This means a lot."

"You've proved yourself worthy over the past few months, and personally, I knew Slammer wanted you in, brother. We all did," I said. "It was a unanimous vote."

His face was full of emotion. "Thank you. I won't let you down."

"I know you won't," I replied, and then looked around the table. There were eleven of us now, and two prospects that had been picked up over the course of four months. I'd made Raptor my Vice President, Horse was now the Road Captain, and Hoss was the Sergeant-At-Arms. Chopper was still my Intelligence Officer, and Buck was the Treasurer and Secretary. "We've got a strong and loyal family. Which brings me to the next thing on the agenda."

Tail put the cut on quickly and sat down next to Horse.

"I spoke to Bastard and he knows whose van it was that dropped off Slammer's killer," I said, feeling my blood begin to boil again. "A man named Cole Johnson. Apparently, he's a prospect for the Devil's Rangers, the Davenport Chapter."

"No surprise there," said Raptor, rubbing a hand over his face.

"I say we go find the piece of shit right now."

"No shit," I answered.

"What's with the girl?" asked Horse. "I mean, why'd they get a fucking woman to do it?"

"I'm not really sure," I said. "Maybe because they're a bunch of cowardly assholes who know we don't go after women for club retaliation."

"Someone's obviously gotta pay," said Hoss. "So, are we going after Cole?"

"We're going to the top," I said. "We get our hands on the girl or Cole, at the very least, and make them talk. Then we take out the one who ordered the hit. I'm sure it was their president or someone higher up."

"Are we limited with what we can do to make that happen?" asked Hoss, tracing circles on the table.

"You talking torture?" I asked with a smirk. I loved Hoss, but he did have a dark side to him that was questionable.

He shrugged. "I'm talking about making it unpleasant for them. Yes."

Some of the guys laughed.

"As far as Cole goes, I don't fucking care. You use whatever methods necessary. He's free game. And shit, I know that we can't kill the girl, but you do what you need to in order to make her talk, if you find out who she is."

"Frankly, I'm shocked that we're not allowed to kill the woman who took out your old man," said Hoss. "That's a kick to the balls, if you ask me. The bitch deserves to die."

26

"I know," I said, wanting to spill her blood, too. "But the Gold Vipers do not kill women, unless… you're standing at the end of their gun barrel, and it's kill or be killed."

"That can be arranged," said Hoss, smirking. "Hers might not be loaded, but I'd be happy to hand a gun to her."

"No," said Raptor. "As much as we'd all like to make this girl pay for Slammer's death, we have to play by the rules. The hit was obviously ordered because of the war that keeps escalating. All I can say is that those fucking cowards have sunk to a new low by using women for their dirty work."

"No shit," said Chopper.

"Someone will pay, and again… it needs to be the person who actually made the call," I emphasized.

"Obviously, it was someone close to Reaper," said Raptor.

"That's what I'm thinking, but we'll get our hands on the shooter so she can confirm it," I said, my palms itching to do it myself.

"What if she refuses to talk?" asked Tail.

"Believe me," I said, smiling coldly. "That bitch won't be in the position to refuse anything. Now, this is how it's going to be – Raptor and Hoss, you bring me Cole Johnson, alive."

"You said he's with the Davenport charter?" asked Hoss.

"That's what I've been told," I said.

"We'll find him," said Raptor. "In fact, we'll leave here right after the meeting."

"Good. Then, let's wrap this up because I'm finished here. Does anyone else have any other business they need to bring to the table?" I asked, looking around.

Nobody did.

The thought suddenly occurred to me that we didn't vote on actually killing the person who ordered the hit on Slammer. I could feel the unspoken agreement around the room, however. We all wanted justice, and this time, it meant death.

"Meeting adjourned," I said, hitting the table with the gavel.

FOUR

RAINA

"**D**ON'T EVEN START on me," I told Marie, holding my hand up as I passed by her in the bar on my way to the breakroom.

She didn't say anything, but gave me a dirty look.

My phone rang. It was Cole.

I answered. "What's up? I'm just about to start my shift."

"Just wanted to let you know that I'm not going to make it back into town today." He took a puff of his cigarette. "Shit didn't turn out like we'd planned."

"Is everything okay?"

"Oh, yeah. Nothing to concern yourself with, Rainy. It's all good."

I smiled at his nickname for me. Rainy. It had been a while since I'd heard it. "Where are you?"

"Just on a road-trip with a couple of brothers. I'll give you a call later tonight."

"Okay. Drive safely and stay out of trouble."

"Thanks, and right back at you."

I hung up and ran into Sal, who was coming out of his office.

"There she is," he said with a twinkle in his eyes. He was dressed in his usual attire – a white collared shirt, the sleeves pushed to his elbows, and black trousers. As usual, his comb-over was glossy from the amount of hairspray he used, and his stomach looked like he'd give birth any day now. Unfortunately, Sal was an alcoholic and by nine o'clock in the evening, the man was usually passed out on the sofa in his office.

"Hi, Sal," I said, noticing how pasty his skin looked. "You feel okay?"

31

"Oh, I'm fine."

"You look a little peaked. You're not running a temperature or anything, are you?" I asked, putting my hand to his forehead.

"I told you I'm fine," he said, shooing my hand away.

"Okay," I said, frowning. "You really should take better care of yourself, you know. Have you been drinking those bottled smoothies still?"

He rolled his eyes. "When I get a chance. They're damn expensive, though."

"That's because they're good for you. You can't put a price on your health, you know," I answered. I knew they were pricey, but he was single and could afford it.

"You can when you've got a lot of bills to pay," he muttered. "Anyway, Nurse Betty, do me a favor and stop by my office on your way to the front. I have some things to discuss with you."

This was a first. He normally didn't bring anyone back there. It was where he escaped to drink privately. I stared hard at his face and noticed that he was completely sober. This was also a first. "Sure. What's it about?"

"Just some business stuff."

"Is it about me being late? I won't let it happen again."

"No. I'm not angry about that. This is something else."

"Okay. I'll be in in a minute." I frowned. "What about Marie? She's going to be pissed if I don't get out there."

"Don't worry about it. I already told Marie we were going to have a discussion when you got here. Her shift isn't over for another twenty minutes, so as far as I'm concerned, she doesn't have anything to complain about."

"Okay."

He turned around and walked back into his office.

Curious as to what he wanted to talk to me about, I hurried into the back where the lockers were, locked my purse up, and headed to Sal's office.

"Okay," I said, sitting down. "What's up?"

Sal, who was sitting behind his desk, put his hands out in front of him. They were shaking and much worse than usual.

"Jesus," I said, staring at them. "Have you gotten this checked out yet?"

He put them down. "As a matter of fact, I did. This morning I went and seen my physician."

I stared at him in disbelief. I'd been harping on him for months to go see a doctor and he'd been giving me crap about it. "What did they say?"

He reached into his desk and pulled out a bottle of vodka. "They took some tests but you and I both know what it's all about. I've been lying to myself for too long, Raina, and the shit is finally catching up to me."

"It's your liver," I said, matter-of-factly.

He removed the cap and took a swig of the bottle. "Yep," he said, wiping his mouth. "That's what they think. I've known it for a while. Probably going to need a new one, but the hell if I'm going to get in line for one."

Frustrated, I grabbed the bottle, before he could take another drink. "If it's your liver, then why are you still drinking?"

"Why shouldn't I? I've got nothing else to live for," he said

33

evenly.

I sat up straighter, shocked at his attitude. "What in the hell are you talking about? You've got me and Cole," I said angrily. "You also have this bar and all of your customers and friends. They come here because of you and what you've created. You can't give up, Sal. I won't let you."

He just stared at me.

Upset, I went on. "Are you even hearing what I'm saying? You're only fifty-five and that's too young to throw your life away."

Finally, he spoke up. "How old are you, Raina? Twenty-five next month, right?"

"Yes, but –"

"You've given up and you're still a young woman with every-thing ahead of you. Hell, if you don't think life is worth living, then I may as well keep drinking," he said, reaching below his desk again. This time, he pulled out a bottle of spiced rum.

"Stop it," I snapped, trying to grab the other bottle. "This isn't funny."

"Do you see me smiling?"

I knew what he was doing. "If you're trying to make a point, I get it, okay? But, it's different. I lost my little boy. He's dead. So is my husband," I said, trying to fight the tears. "It's so damn hard…"

"I know what hard is. I lost my wife Carol to cancer before you were born. Loved that woman. She was everything to me. I also lost my sister, your mother. If I would have given up though, Raina, you and your brother would have ended up in foster care somewhere."

"I'm not dying, Sal," I argued. *I just didn't care about living anymore.*

"Bullshit. You may not be dying, but you certainly aren't living.

34

I can see it in your eyes, Raina."

"What do you expect me to do, Sal?" I argued. "It's not like I can go and get my son replaced like a damn liver." I knew that it was cruel, but I was angrier than hell. "He's gone. I don't have another chance at getting him back."

"Maybe not, but you have a chance to make a difference in somebody else's life, Raina. Just like I did for you and Cole. It may not be today or tomorrow, but you will. Believe me."

"If we made so much of a difference, then why have you carried on drinking all of these years when you knew what it was doing to you?"

"Because I lied to myself, sweetheart, and I guess that I didn't think it would ever get this bad. Now I can't even go a few hours without needing a shot of something."

"Can't you get medical treatment?" I asked, so frightened of losing him, too.

"I could, although I don't know if it's worth it," he replied. "Once they get the test results back, I know what they're going to say."

I stared at his skin, really noticing the yellowish tinge for the first time. "It's worth it. You have to hang in there, and for God's sake," I leaned over his desk and snatched away the bottle. "Stop drinking!"

"It's not easy. Lord knows I tried a couple of times these last few months, and the withdrawals are horrible. But," he looked me square in the eye, "I'm willing to get help if you're willing to do it, too."

I grunted. "Who in the hell can help me get my son back?"

"Nobody, but someone can help you learn to live without him," he answered. "I'm talking about counseling."

"I don't want to live without him," I said, my voice breaking.

He grabbed my hand and squeezed. "Part of him will always be with you," said Sal. "But you need to learn how to move on. You need to see a grief counselor."

I turned my face away and brushed at the tears. "So, if I agree to talk to someone, you'll agree to get treatment for your liver?"

He nodded.

"Okay," I replied, willing to do anything to help Sal. *I could even just pretend to go*, I thought. "I'll check around and make an appointment. You, on the other hand, can't wait."

"I know. My doctor is waiting for me to call him back so he can refer me to a treatment center. I wanted to talk to you first."

"Treatment center. That's good. You're going to go through with it, though, right?"

"I will. As long as you agree to talk to someone, too. In fact," Sal reached into his back pocket and pulled out his wallet. He opened it up and pulled out a business card. "You can call this woman, Janene Bakerson."

I stared down at the card. So much for pretending. "So, she specializes in grief therapy, huh?"

He nodded.

"I don't know what good it's going to do," I mumbled. "But, if it's the only way you're willing to get treatment, I'll do it."

He looked relieved. "Thank you, sweetheart."

I put the card in my back pocket and stood up. "Make that call to your doctor, Sal. I want to know that you're serious about this."

"I'm serious, which brings me to another reason why I need to talk to you. Sit back down."

Sighing, I did.

"When I'm gone, I'm going to need you to take over the bar."

"Me? What about Lana?" Lana was his manager.

"She's not family. I need you to run the place. She'll still be your manager, if you want her."

"Lana is not going to be happy. Why don't you just let her run the place until you get back? I don't want to get everyone here pissed off." Plus, the thought of taking on so much at once sounded exhausting.

"I'm not coming back," he said, smiling grimly. "I'm an alcoholic. I can't surround myself with booze if I have any kind of a chance at succeeding."

"Oh, hell," I groaned. "I can't run this place, Sal. I don't have what it takes to do something like this."

He scowled at me. "Bullshit. You have what it takes. I believe in you and that's why I'm offering."

The only thing I believed in at the moment was that there wasn't much left in the world *to* believe in. But I didn't want Sal to die. He may have been a weak man when it came to alcohol, but he was a good man.

"What about Cole? Why don't you see if he can help out?" The suggestion sounded ridiculous, even to me. He was too involved with the Devil's Rangers.

"Bring him in to help if you want. But, you know as well as I do, that his priorities are all messed up. Honestly, you're the only person I trust running the bar. You know what I always say   'there is nothing like family'. Nothing. We need stick together."

37

"I hear you… but Sal, I don't know diddly-squat about running a place like this," I said, my knee bouncing a mile a minute from nerves. Not only that, I didn't know if I could handle the pressure at the moment.

"What are you talking about? You practically grew up here. Hell, I remember when you were a teenager, you helped with the books and even gave me suggestions when I hired some of the staff. As far as I'm concerned, you know more than anyone else, even Lana. Hell, I would have made you manager a long time ago, but you were needed at home."

For Billy…

"We need each other," he said, as if reading my mind. "Please, Raina."

I looked up. "You know I'd do anything for you, Sal. If this is what you want, I'll do my best."

His eyes widened in surprise. "Really?"

I leaned forward and gave him the stink-eye. "As long as you get your ass into treatment; I'll do whatever you want me to do."

Smiling, he patted my hand. "That's my girl. We'll talk more about it later this evening. When Matt comes in."

Matt was one of the newer bartenders.

"Okay. Just let me know if you need a ride to the clinic when the time comes," I said, standing up.

"I'd like that," he replied, his eyes getting watery.

Feeling a little choked up myself again, I picked up the two bottles of booze and headed toward the door.

"By the way, tell Marie to stop back here. I'm going to tell her the news."

I turned around and smiled. Even though I'd love to see the expression on her face, I didn't want to be there when he told her. She was going to flip out. "Okay."

Knowing the animosity between us, he smiled. "This is your place now, honey. You can fire and hire whoever you want. Just make sure it makes sense, of course."

"You sure you about that?" I asked.

He placed a hand on his stomach. "You're the one who has to work with them. Anyway, I'd expect the co-owner of the bar to have a say in who works here and who doesn't."

I stared at him in surprise. "Co-owner? I thought you just wanted me to run the place."

"You know that when I'm gone, the bar will be yours and Cole's, anyway. Fifty-fifty."

I hadn't really thought about that.

"So, you may as well get your hands dirty now. See if it's something you want to keep going. When I'm gone, you two can keep this bar or sell it. Having you run the place now will give you a taste of what you might be giving up if you sold it, though."

"Let's not talk about that," I said. "If you get your ass in treatment, you could be around for another thirty or forty years."

"Oh hell," he said, waving his hand. "I don't want to live that long."

"Sal, you were the one who was just going on about life having a purpose..."

"I know. That doesn't mean I want to live to be eighty years old," he said, pulling out a cigar from the humidor sitting on his desk.

My eyes widened.

He sniffed it. "What? If I'm going to be sober for the rest of my life, I'm smoking this last Cuban."

Shaking my head and smiling, I turned around and left his office.

FIVE

TANK

RAPTOR AND HOSS called me a few hours later to give me an update on Cole Johnson. They'd left their cuts behind and had taken a cage out to Davenport to avoid being spotted by the Devil's Rangers.

"We haven't been able to locate him, but he has a sister who works over at Sal's."

"The bar here in Jensen?" I asked, surprised. It was a shit-hole, from what I'd remembered. "Isn't that the place Mavis used to hang out?"

"Yeah," muttered Raptor. "That's the place."

"So, where's Cole? Anyone know?"

"No. We found the location of their clubhouse and hung around the area for a while. We even followed two of their club bitches to a bar up the street and bought them a couple of drinks. Told them we were interested in becoming prospects for the Devil's Rangers. Said we knew Cole."

"They believe you?"

"Hell yeah. That's how we found out about his sister. Apparently, Cole is on the road at the moment and won't be back for a few days."

I sighed. "Okay. Did you find an address to where he lives?"

"No. Just got intel on the sister. Her name is Raina Davis"

"Raina Davis, huh?" I replied. "The name sounds familiar. Did she ever come to one of our parties?"

"Not that I'm aware of," said Raptor.

"I've heard the name before. It's not that common. I just don't know where," I replied, racking my brain to come up with something. I wondered if I'd banged the chick in the past, and that's

43

why she sounded familiar.

"You want us to check out Sal's?" he asked.

"No. I'll take care of it myself." I needed to see Raina Davis for myself. See if she jogged any memories.

"You sure you want to do that?"

I frowned. "What do you mean, am I sure?"

Raptor sighed. "You're pissed off, for good reason, but this needs to be handled carefully. You don't want to frighten her. She'll alert her brother."

I closed my eyes and rubbed the bridge of my nose. "I'm going to play it cool. I'm not an idiot."

"I realize that, but you have a personal vendetta, just like I did with Adriana, and we both know that I was a raging bull."

"I hear you, brother. Don't worry; I'm just going to feel her out. See if she'll open up to me about Cole. I'll put on the old Tank charm and have her eating out of my hand." And hell, maybe off of my dick, too. The thought of making Cole Johnson's sister get down on her knees was giving me wood and I had yet to meet the bitch.

"Good. Take that route. I'm thinking that if she works at a dive like Sal's, chances are the girl is butt-ugly and will welcome a little flirting."

"When I'm done with her, I'll know her entire family history, her social security number, and whether or not she likes it up the ass."

Raptor chuckled. "I have no doubt, brother."

"Seriously, though, she might even have information on the shooter. Hell, maybe she is the shooter. Did either of those gutter sluts mention whether or not Raina was mixed up with the club?"

"It doesn't sound like she wants any part of their club. They talked about her like she was a stuck-up bitch. One of them even called her a 'cunt'."

"Interesting. Now I really need to see this cunt for myself. I'm going to head over to Sal's now. I'll call you."

"Sounds good. Hoss and I will head back to the clubhouse. Remember – this needs to be handled delicately."

Even now that I was club president, Raptor still didn't trust me to keep my shit together.

He knew me too well…

"Hey, relax. I can be as delicate as a fucking flower when I need to be," I said, smirking

"Yeah. I know. Just like a Venus-fucking-flytrap. Just be careful, someone might recognize you at Sal's."

"I won't be wearing my cut."

"You'd better do more than that to change your appearance. I'm serious. You're going to stick out like a sore thumb. The place is a shit-hole. Someone's going to make you."

I sighed. "I hear you and don't worry, I got it under control."

AFTER MARIE LEARNED the news, I expected her to storm out of the bar, spitting bullets. Instead, she surprised the hell out of me.

"Congratulations on your new position," she said on her way out. "I heard the news."

I forced a smile. "Thanks," I said, realizing that she was probably worried about losing her job.

"So, I was wondering if we could go over my schedule later? I'd like to make some changes, if it's at all possible?"

"Sure. We can talk about it," I said, grabbing the clipboard with our schedules from under the bar. "Are you wanting to add more hours?" Right now she worked Tuesdays, Thursdays, and Saturday nights.

"Actually, I was thinking more that I'd cut back some of my late nights."

"You only work one now as it is," I said, frowning.

She smiled. "Yeah. It's just not working for me anymore."

I worked Friday and Sunday nights. "Maybe you and I could switch a day? I'll work Saturday nights and you can have my Friday nights?"

Her smile fell. "No. That won't work either."

I sighed. "Okay. How about you take my Sunday nights instead and I work your Saturdays?" That would mean two busy nights in a row, but my weekends were now as free as a bird.

"No. I could work first shift on Friday?"

"Matt already does," I said, getting frustrated.

"Oh. That's right. Well, I'm sure we'll come up with something," she said, giving me a big smile. "I've got to get to my nail appointment."

"I guess we will have to, or you'll just have to look for a job that fits into your schedule a little better."

Her smile fell. "I don't want to work anywhere else."

I shrugged. "Then you're going to have to stick with your current hours or talk to Matt and see if he'll be willing to switch your Saturday night. I doubt it, though. He works another job on the weekends."

"I see this is going to be a fucking treat," she mumbled, picking up her purse.

I bit back a smile. "What was that?"

"Nothing. I'd better get going. See you tomorrow afternoon."

"Okay." I watched her walk away, a feeling of dread already working its way into my stomach. I knew that I was going to have to either be firm with Marie or fire her. I preferred the latter, but wasn't ready to jump into doing interviews.

Matt arrived thirty minutes later; Sal spoke to him before he started his shift. When he stepped out of Sal's office, I could tell he had a lot on his mind.

"First of all, congratulations," he said, smiling. "I think it's great that you're going to be in charge now."

"Thanks," I said, still unsure of the changes myself. I had so many emotions running through me and was beginning to crave a cigarette. I hadn't smoked in three years, though, and money was tight. "I wish it were under different circumstances."

"I know." He sighed. "Is Sal going to be okay?"

"I hope so," I replied. "At least he's getting help."

We'd talked about Sal's drinking before. Matt's ex-wife was an alcoholic and had gone through treatment a couple of times.

He nodded. "How about you? How are you doing?"

I shrugged. "Okay, I guess. I'm more worried about him, I guess, than anything else now."

"I was thinking that after we close down the bar, you might want to go for breakfast?" he asked. "Maybe Charlie's?"

Charlie's was a diner up the street that was open twenty-four hours.

I was about to refuse, but my tongue had other ideas. "Sure."

He grinned. "Good."

Not sure what in the hell I was thinking, I told him that it was probably a good idea, considering all of the changes that were happening. "Maybe we should invite Peggy, too?" I asked. Peggy was the server scheduled for that evening.

His smile faltered. "Sure, if you'd like."

I knew she probably wouldn't join us, but I wanted him to know that it wasn't going to be a date. We'd already gone there and I wasn't feeling up to trying it again. At least, anytime soon.

When Matt had first started working at the bar, we'd flirted innocently and then one night, after my car wouldn't start, he ended up giving me a ride home. We shared a bottle of wine and then ended up on my sofa, making out, until Billy had woken up, needing a glass of water. It had been a little awkward afterward. Matt had gone home and we'd pretended that the episode on my sofa had never happened. Then, a week later he told me that he and his ex, Connie, were trying to work things out. That was five months ago. Since then, things had grown sour between the two of them again and I had my

49

own problems. I had to admit, I still found him attractive. With his light brown hair and kind eyes, he reminded me of a young Kevin Costner. But, the last thing I wanted was to get involved with Matt, whether it was physical or emotional.

Sal walked out of the back. "Raina, could I talk to you for a few minutes?"

"Of course," I replied

"I'll go and check on Monty over there. See if he needs another drink," said Matt, nodding toward a regular at the end of the bar. It was still early and there were only a handful of customers.

"Check and see if he wants a pizza," I said. "He mentioned possibly ordering one."

"Okay," Matt replied.

I walked into Sal's office.

"I'm taking the rest of the day off," he said in a low voice. "To get some of my things in order, before I actually do put myself into treatment."

I could smell the booze on him and my stomach knotted up. "Do you want me to drive you?"

"No, I'm fine."

I let out a ragged sigh. "You've been drinking some more."

"Honey, I told you before, stopping cold-turkey is hard. But, I promise you – I'm going to try my best to get away from it. But not until I have my stuff in order. I can barely function when I'm stone-cold sober."

I crossed my arms under my chest and frowned.

He patted me on top of the head. "Raina, don't worry, okay? I'm

50

not drunk. In fact, I'm waiting for Eddie to come and pick me up. He's going to help me fill out some legal paperwork that's needed for the bar."

Eddie was his lawyer and a long-time friend.

I relaxed. "Okay."

"If you need anything, call me."

"And you call me when you find out more about enrolling into a treatment program."

"I will. I promise." His cell phone went off and he looked at it. "Oh, it's Eddie. He's waiting for me outside. I'll give you a call later, honey."

"Okay, Sal. Take care."

He put his phone away. "You, too," he said, before kissing me on the cheek and heading out.

I watched him leave, and although I hoped Sal was going to be okay, I wasn't going to hold my breath for it. Hope had abandoned me too many times already.

SEVEN

TANK

BEFORE HITTING SAL'S, I stopped back home and replaced my cut with a blue V-neck cotton shirt and added a baseball cap, just to play it safe. I then drove my black Sierra Denali and parked it up the street from the bar. When I walked inside of the place, I was a little surprised. It was packed for a Tuesday night and many of the customers were jocks and dressed in baseball uniforms. It was loud, people were having fun, and it certainly wasn't the hole-in-the-wall I'd been expecting. It definitely reminded me more of a sports bar.

"Hey, man, what can I get you?" asked the bartender, a friendly-looking guy in his twenties.

"Michelob," I replied, sitting down at the end of the bar next to an old man eating popcorn and watching a game on one of the big screen televisions. We nodded at each other.

"Bottled or tap?" asked the bartender.

"Bottled," I replied, looking around. "This place is busy."

The bartender nodded. "Yeah, it has been hopping ever since Sal remodeled a couple of months ago and did some advertising. He's also sponsoring a baseball team this year."

"Huh," I replied, taking it all in. I'd never been in the bar itself, but it was obvious the place had been newly renovated. "You only have the one waitress working?"

"No, we have Claire, who's out having a smoke," he replied.

The other one was serving a table full of baseball players. The woman was a short, middle-aged blonde. Not exactly the sister I had in mind for Cole, but I wasn't about to rule her out either.

The bartender reached into the cooler and pulled out a cold one. "Here you go."

"Thanks," I said, pushing a ten dollar bill toward him.

He walked over to the register and took out the change.

"Keep it," I said, taking a swig of beer.

"Thanks," he said, eyeing me curiously. "So, is this your first time here?"

"Why do you ask?"

"No reason," he said quickly. "Just get mostly regulars here during the week."

"I don't look like a regular?" I asked, smirking.

"No, you look like that wrestler," piped in the old man with a toothless smile. "What in the hell is his name? Oh, yeah… Randy Orton."

I grunted. "Hell, I wish I was Orton."

"So do I," said the old geezer. "I'd make you buy me a beer. What's your name anyway?"

"Justin," I said, giving him my real name.

"I'm Gordy and that there's Matt," he answered, nodding toward the bartender. "Oh, and there's Raina, coming out of the kitchen." He lowered his voice. "Check out the tatas on that one."

I jerked my head around and found myself staring at a girl heading toward us carrying a small pizza. She was medium height with raven hair and bright blue eyes.

"Here you go, Gordy," she said, setting it down in front of him. "It's right out of the oven, so you'd better let it cool before digging in this time."

"Thanks, *mom*," he said, staring more at her chest than the pizza. I had to admit, her curves were impressive and owning a strip-joint, I'd seen a lot.

She pushed her hair behind her ears. "Just looking out for you. Last week you burnt your tongue and we had to hear about it for the rest of the night."

"That's 'cause it hurt like hell," he said. "Should have warned me about that pizza oven of yours."

"She did warn you," said Matt, rolling his eyes.

Raina put her hands on her waist. "Which reminds me, you never paid up on that bet we had."

"Which bet was that?" asked, Gordy.

"The one where I warned you that the pizza was too hot to eat. You bet me a dollar that you could handle it."

"I don't recall betting any money on it," he said, blowing on the pizza.

"You're really going to squelch on another bet?" Raina answered, smirking.

"You'd better pay up," said Matt. "'Cause you definitely lost that bet."

Gordy looked up at Raina. "I've got your payment. In fact, it's your lucky day now that my tongue is healed. You sit on it and we'll call it even." He stuck his tongue out and wiggled it lewdly.

She shuddered. "How about I pay you to put it away?"

"Dude, you need to work on your technique if your tongue rides are only worth a buck," I said, taking another swig of beer.

Raina laughed and Matt pulled out another bottle from the cooler. "This one's on me. That comment deserves it," he said, setting another beer in front of me.

"Works for me. Thanks," I said and then looked at Raina, who was eyeing me curiously. "That pizza looks good. You have any more of those in back?"

"Uh, sure. What kind do you like?"

"What do you have?" I asked, checking her out. She was definitely a looker, reminding me a lot of the actress Megan Fox.

She licked her lips. "Sausage, pepperoni, or deluxe. That's about it. They're just frozen, though. Nothing to write home about."

"They're damn good though," said Gordy, picking up a piece of his. "I'd give you some of mine but I'm too hungry."

"That's okay, because I'm starving myself." I looked back over at Raina. "Why don't you pick one out for me?"

She looked surprised. "Me? I don't even know what you like."

"Sure you do. I'm easy," I said, giving her a little smile.

Gordy laughed. "Hell, for Raina... we can all be easy."

"Get him a deluxe," said Matt, looking a little jealous. I wondered if the two of them had something going.

"Actually, get me two of those. Please, darlin'? I have a big appetite," I said, standing up and stretching my legs.

She gave me the once-over and then quickly looked away. "Sure thing."

"Where's your bathroom?" I asked. "I'd like to wash my hands."

Raina cleared her throat. "I'll show you."

"Thank you," I said as she began walking away.

As much as I wanted to kill her brother, I couldn't help but admire her perky little ass. I decided that Cole owed me bigtime, and besides slitting his throat, part of the payment would definitely be a piece of Raina.

"So, two deluxe pizzas?" she said, looking back at me over her shoulder.

"Yes, please. Unless you're getting off of work soon and want to join me for some real pizza?"

She stopped abruptly and turned around. "Excuse me?"

EIGHT

RAINA

I STARED UP AT the tattooed stranger and my breath suddenly caught in my throat. I hadn't realized how big he was until now. Tall, broad shoulders, and arm muscles that could break someone's neck easily during a choke-hold.

"Rocco's is a few blocks from here. Their pizza is rated the best in the city," he said. "I've always wanted to try it out. You game?"

"You're asking me out?" I replied, flattered and yet irritated. He was hot; there was no doubt about it. He also looked like he wanted to devour me whole with that hungry gaze. But, I wasn't in the mood for a one-night stand, and I was pretty sure it was all the he wanted. "Just like that?"

His smile was disarming. "From where I'm standing, nothing about you is 'just like that'."

I blushed, in spite of everything. This guy was definitely trouble and there'd been a time when I'd have met it head-on. That person was long gone. "How many times have you used that dorky line?"

His smile never wavered. "First night this week. By the way, you may not know this but... I'm Batman."

I laughed. "Enough."

"Did the sun come up or did you just smile at me?"

From the twinkle in his pale green eyes, I could see that he was thoroughly enjoying this. "Do any of these lines ever work?"

"Of course. Only because I'm the one saying them, and admit it, you're already finding me fascinating. I can see it in the way you're undressing me with your eyes. Did I mention that I was Batman?"

I laughed again. "What you are is crazy."

"Sorry, beautiful women bring that out in me, and that's not a line. It's the truth. So, what do you say? Join me later?"

"I don't even know your name."

"It's Justin. What's yours?"

"Raina." I sighed. "To be honest, I already have plans after my shift. Besides, when I get off of work, I'm sure it will be well past your bedtime."

His eyebrow arched. "My bedtime?"

I nodded toward his body, which I had no doubt was amazing underneath those clothes. "A guy like you probably turns in at a reasonable hour, so you have the energy to keep up your... fitness regime," I said, not really knowing what to call it. It was obvious that he spent hours pumping iron. It made me wonder if he was some kind of professional bodybuilder or fitness instructor. I had to admit he looked damn good, but sex wasn't something I wanted right now and guys like this weren't interested in long, deep conversations.

"Number one, some of my best workouts are done in bed. Number two, I doubt I could sleep knowing that you've already made plans with another guy."

I laughed. "I don't even know how to respond to that."

"Say you'll go out with me and cancel your other date."

"It's not a date," I said quickly and then wondered why I'd bothered to clarify that for him.

He grinned. "Even better."

"I'm sorry. I can't cancel," I said. "It's a business meeting. So, do you want me to throw in the two pizzas still?"

Justin gave me a scorned puppy-dog look and shoved his hands into his pockets. "Sure. A man's gotta eat."

I laughed at the way he was drawing an imaginary line with his shoe, pouting like a schoolboy. "Stop. You really are pathetic."

He tilted his head. "If I do, will you agree to have dinner with me tomorrow at Axel's, instead?"

Axel's was an expensive steakhouse. I'd been there once and the prices had been outrageous.

I smiled sadly. "I really can't."

"Can't or won't?"

Looking around, I moved closer to him. "As much as I'd love to join you, it's just not a good time for me right now. My life is a mess and there is too much going on here at work," I said softly, wishing for a moment that everything was different. But, it was what it was.

His penetrating gaze probed mine. "A mess. We have a lot in common."

"Oh?"

"Sometimes the only way you can fix a mess is by creating another one. I'm just trying to decide if it's going to bite me in the ass later," he said, running a finger along the side of my arm.

I shivered and took a step back. "I don't understand."

He smiled again, but it didn't quite reach his eyes. "I know. Anyway, I hope things start getting better for you. In the meantime," he said, looking over my head toward the bar, "I think I'm going to take a raincheck on the pizzas."

Surprised, I asked why.

"You reminded me of some other things that I need to take care of. I need to head out."

"I'm sorry. I didn't mean to scare you off," I said, forcing a smile.

"Don't worry. I'm not one who scares easily," he said with a wink.

"I can tell."

"I'm going to finish my beer and take off. It was nice talking to you, Raina."

"Uh, yeah. Same here."

He turned around and walked into the bathroom. As I watched the way he moved, I wasn't sure why, but his swagger seemed familiar. Shrugging it off, I turned around and went back to the bar.

"Looks like you two were having a deep conversation over there," remarked Matt when I returned.

"Not really," I said. "I asked him what kind of pizza he wanted and we just got to talking."

"So, what did he decide on?"

"He changed his mind on the pizza. Said he was going to finish his beer and leave."

"Excuse me, can I order one of those pizzas?" asked a new customer who had seated himself on the other side of Gordy. He was a mechanic from across the street and a regular.

I turned to him. "Sure, Jay. What kind would you like?"

"Pepperoni," he said. "Is that Tank you were talking to?"

"Tank?" I repeated, writing down his pizza order. "What are you talking about?"

"That guy you were talking to over by the bathrooms. I swear, that's got to be him."

"I'm not sure who Tank is, but that guy's name was Justin," I answered.

"I'm sure you're right. He's not wearing a cut and I doubt he'd be over on this side of town."

"What do you mean, a cut?" asked Matt.

"You know, it's what those bikers usually wear," piped in Gordy. "Displaying the name of their club. They put those patches on them."

"That's right. Your brother Cole is mixed up with the Devil's Rangers, isn't he?" asked Matt.

I couldn't answer. I felt like the wind had been knocked out of me. There'd been something familiar about Justin, and hadn't Cole mentioned the name Tank before? I wasn't sure.

Matt frowned. "Are you okay, Raina? You look like a ghost."

"I need to make a phone call," I said quickly. "I'll be back."

"Okay," he answered.

I raced to the breakroom and tried calling Cole again. This time, he answered.

"Hey, Raina. What's up?"

"There's a big guy in here with tats and muscles. He's not wearing a cut, but one of our regulars thinks he looks like a guy named Tank."

Cole swore. "Raina, you need to get your ass out of the bar, now."

"Who is he?" I whispered, now shaking.

"Tank is Slammer's son. The new president of the Gold Vipers."

I almost dropped my phone.

NINE
TANK

W HEN I MADE it out of the men's room and back up to the bar, Raina was nowhere to be seen.

Fuck.

"It is you," said a newcomer seated next to Gordy. I'd noticed him by the bar when I'd been talking to Raina. He'd been staring at me and I'd wondered if he'd recognized me. Apparently, he had.

"Sorry, have we met?" I asked.

The guy looked disappointed. "I did some work on your old man's truck last year. Dropped it off at the clubhouse and we had a beer together. Surprised you don't remember. The name is Jay."

"That's right." I chugged downed the rest of my Michelob.

"How is he, by the way?" asked Jay.

Surprised that he hadn't heard, I lied and told him that Slammer was fine. "Where'd Raina go?" I asked, searching the bar.

"She went to the breakroom," said Matt, studying me with piercing scrutiny. "So, they call you Tank?"

"Sometimes," I said, frustrated. My cover was blown to hell and Raina was probably calling her brother Cole. *If* she knew who I was. "Catch yeah later."

I walked out the front door of the bar, pulled my gun out of my ankle holster, and raced around to the employee exit, which was on the other side of the building. I wasn't sure what I was going to do, but knew that this could be my last chance to talk to her. As I approached the back door, I heard the screeching of tires and turned to see a silver four-door sedan peel away.

TEN

RAINA

I SAW JUSTIN IN my rearview mirror as I raced out of the parking lot. He was standing next to the back door and would have clearly intercepted me had I left even a few seconds later.

Shit. Shit. Shit.

My heart was pounding and my hands shook as I drove blindly through the streets, not sure where to go. Justin knew where I worked. Who I was. What I'd done to his father.

Why else would he be there?

There was no doubt in my mind that he would have killed me if I'd have gone on that date. I imagined his hands around my throat, choking the life out of me, and my eyes filled with tears. I was fucking dead.

My cell phone rang, making me jump.

"It's me," said Cole, when I picked it up. "Are you okay?"

"Yes," I said, trying to compose myself. I didn't need him to hear me crying. "For now."

"Jesus Christ, I knew killing Slammer was a bad idea. And now those fuckers know you did it. This is bad, Raina. Really fucking bad."

"Yeah, I get it. How do you think they find out?" I asked, my eyes darting to the mirror again.

"I didn't say anything but obviously, somebody recognized the van and put two-and-two together. You've got to get out of town. Or better yet, I'll call my Prez and get you some club protection."

"I'm not getting help from the Devil's Rangers," I snapped. "I trust them as much as I trust the Gold Vipers."

"Why can't you give them a break? They're on our side."

"Don't even start with me."

He sighed. "Fine. Then get your ass out of town. In fact, why don't you call Sal and tell him that you need to hide out at his place for a while."

"Are you fucking kidding me? He's going to want to know why. I can't tell him that I shot some biker club's president," I snapped. "He's got enough shit on his plate right now as it is."

"What are you talking about?"

I checked the rearview mirror again and was relieved to find I still wasn't being followed. "Sal thinks he has liver disease and is going into treatment. I tried calling you earlier, to tell you about it, but you wouldn't answer."

"I'm doing a job right now. He's got liver disease? Is he going to die?" he asked, sounding worried.

"Let's hope not. What kind of a job?"

"I can't say. It's club business."

"Great," I mumbled. "I'm sure it's totally legal, too."

"You're the last person who should be giving me shit. Besides, if it wasn't for these guys, I'd have nothing."

"You'd have nothing?! Do realize that if it wasn't for your club, Billy would still be alive?" I cried, angry and frustrated. "That we'd both have *him*?"

"It's wasn't their fault that Billy was shot. It was the Gold Vipers. Those crazy motherfucking cowards sprayed the party with bullets."

"Yeah, and that's the kind of life you really want? Being part of a club with those kinds of enemies?"

"You don't know them the way that I do. They're my friends. My brothers. We'd die for each other."

"You're only a prospect. They make you do the shit they don't want to do – and for what? So you can wear their colors someday and end up in jail or six feet under?"

"You don't understand."

"I understand more than you do obviously. Quit defending them, Cole."

"Look, I gotta go. Drive your ass to Sal's and stay there for the night. Make some shit up about why you have to do it, but go there. Meanwhile, I'll find someplace safe for you to go tomorrow."

"So, I'm supposed to go on the run now?"

"If you're not going to accept protection from the club, then we're going to have to find a different way to keep you alive."

I sighed.

"Don't worry, sis. I'll be back as soon as possible and we'll figure something out. I won't let them hurt you."

"I can't go on the run. Sal needs me right now," I replied.

"You might not have a choice. If Tank is after you, he's not going to stop looking until he finds you."

"He is, huh?"

"He'll hunt you down until the day he dies. He was close to his old man."

"Maybe I should find him before he finds me."

"Are you crazy? Don't do it, Raina. Don't even fucking do it."

"I don't think I have any other choice," I said, hanging up on my brother. He called back and I turned off my cell phone.

ELEVEN

TANK

I HEADED HOME AFTER I called Raptor and filled him in on what had happened over at Sal's.

"She obviously knows of Cole's involvement," he said.

"Yep. And I'm sure that he's now aware that we're on to him."

"Did you try following her?"

"No," I said. "She drove off like a bat out of Hell. I'm working on getting an address for her, though."

"An address, huh? You call Vera?"

"Yeah."

Vera was a girl I'd banged last month after changing her tire on the side of the road. She worked for the IRS and it didn't take much to get intel from her, especially addresses.

"You have to bribe her?"

"Of course. She's going to call be back within an hour. Said she had to slip back into work and log in to the computer."

"Good thing you slipped it to her a few weeks ago. She's certainly been coming in handy."

"I'll be coming in handy later, too," I remarked with sly grin. "The girl has the mouth of a Hoover."

"Glad to see you're finally coming around," said Raptor, sounding amused. "I was getting worried about you, brother."

"I'm just... adjusting," I said, serious again. Knowing my dad was gone still hurt like a son-of-a-bitch. Knowing that revenge was close at hand, made things a little easier to swallow.

"It's good to hear. I know it isn't easy and we're all going to miss him."

71

"Yeah," I replied, feeling my throat tighten.

"We're here for you. *I'm* here for you, brother. You know that, right?"

"Yes. Same to you. I couldn't do any of this without you. I mean it."

"Fuck that. You're the 'Tank', strong-willed and fearless. You're more capable of leading this group than any of us and that's why you were voted in as Prez."

I couldn't help but smile. "You guys make it easy."

"Your crew respects and would do anything for you and know you'd do the same."

"Damn right. I'd take a bullet for any of you."

"And you know that any of us would return the favor."

"Yeah."

We were both silent for a few seconds.

"Anyhow, let me know when you get the address and we'll go talk to her."

"That's okay. I'll handle it," I replied, wanting to see Raina again. I knew she was sister to the enemy, but I couldn't get those eyes out of my head. And those lips. I felt myself grow hard just thinking about them wrapped around my cock.

"What are you going to do?"

"Scare her into telling me where Cole is."

I figured by her reaction, she probably hated me as much as I hated her piece-of-shit brother, but I needed Raina to know the gravity of the situation and that her brother was playing for the wrong team. Nobody shoots my old man and walks away without facing the consequences. If she could persuade her brother to give me the name of the shooter, I might even just let him live with nothing more than a limp.

"You sure?" he asked.

"Yeah."

He let out a long sigh. "Do you think she could have been the shooter?"

"No," I said, remembering the fearful look she'd given me when I'd approached her for a damn date. My gut told me that there wasn't an ounce of evil in that girl. The person who killed Slammer was a ruthless killer. Someone probably propositioned by the Devil's Rangers. "I just don't see it. Cole's sister doesn't seem like a killer."

"You and I both know that what she seems like doesn't mean shit. If this chick did kill your old man, then she won't think twice about shooting you. Don't underestimate her."

"I hear you," I replied. "I can handle this princess, though. I just need to get that address."

TWELVE

RAINA

W ONDERING IF JUSTIN had caused any kind of scene, I turned my phone back on and dialed the bar. Matt answered

"Where'd you go?" he asked. I could hear customers laughing and talking in the background. Sal's was obviously still busy.

"A friend of mine called with an emergency," I lied. "She's in the hospital and needs someone to watch her kids."

"Oh, that's bad news. Hope she's okay," he replied sincerely.

I relaxed. He evidently hadn't noticed anything unusual and Justin must not have said anything.

"Well, it's appendicitis. I'm sorry to do this to you, but I'm not going to be able to make it back in tonight."

"It's okay," he replied. "We've been slammed with customers, but I think we can handle it."

I felt so guilty for leaving them, but I knew that going back to the bar was a death wish. "How's Peggy doing?"

"She has her hands full, but don't worry. We've got it covered."

"Okay. Did Sal stop back in or call?"

"No. I'm sure he's sound asleep by now." He spoke away from the phone. "Hold on, I'll be right with you, sir."

"I'm sure you're right. I'd better let you take care of the customers. I'll call you tomorrow and let you know what's going on."

"Okay. I guess we'll have to reschedule breakfast," he said, sounding disappointed.

"Yes. Next time?"

"Anytime."

"Okay. We'll talk about it later."

"Sounds good."

I said goodbye and hung up. Matt was definitely into me right now. It was probably better that we hadn't gone out for breakfast.

I pulled over to the side of the road and started searching the internet for information on the Gold Vipers and found plenty, including an article about Justin's deceased girlfriend, a woman named Krystal Blake, who was thought to have been murdered by the Devil's Rangers.

"And so it begins," I mumbled, reading further into the story. Unfortunately, no charges were filed on any of the members of the Devil's Rangers and there hadn't been enough DNA evidence to convict anyone, although a biker by the name of Thomas Kramer, nickname Breaker, had been a leading suspect. He was later found dead in his truck, having bled to death by a bullet to the groin. I also found several other articles about Breaker being incarcerated for rape. It was only a couple of months after he was released that the thing with Krystal occurred.

I continued my search and found a couple of other articles in which two leaders of the Devil's Rangers had also died. The first one happened three years ago, in a fire up in Minnesota. The leader of the Hayward Chapter, whose road name was Mud, was found in their clubhouse, charbroiled. The other victim was found with his genitals cut off. He'd been dead before the reported fire had taken place. Again, there was no DNA evidence, although some rogue biker, who called himself The Judge, was still wanted for questioning.

Finally, I found an article that was dated only a few weeks back.

Another Devil's Rangers president had been found dead up in Alaska after some kind of run-in with an FBI agent named Stryker. The man's name had been Jon Hughes and he'd been head of the Mother Chapter, which in the biker world, was apparently a big deal. Both men had been found dead, along with a couple other members of the Devil's Rangers. There weren't any links this time to the Gold Vipers, but it happened around the same time that Billy was killed.

It's gotta be related, I thought. *All of it.*

I started to get dizzy thinking about all of the death and destruction caused by both clubs and knew I had to try talking Cole into running away with me. We had to get as far from Iowa as we possibly could, even if it meant leaving Sal. As far as I was concerned, our being near him was a far more dangerous threat than the liver disease at the moment. But first, I would pay a visit to Slammer's son. I wanted him to know why I'd killed his father and to make sure he left the rest of my family alone for good.

I continued searching until I was forced to use my credit card to get the home address for a Justin Fleming, AKA Tank. I knew where their clubhouse was located, but was too skittish to drive by it. There would be too many bikers hanging around the place and if I was spotted, they'd chase me down and that would be that.

I started the car and began following the directions on my phone to the address, hoping it was correct. When I knew that I was close, I parked two blocks away and took the gun out of my purse. It was the same one I'd killed Slammer with. Cole had warned me to get rid of it, but I'd had too much on my mind. Now, I was glad that I'd kept the damn thing.

Checking the gun to make sure it was loaded, I shoved it back into my purse and got out of the car. I still wasn't sure what the hell I was going to do, but something needed to be done about the guy who'd tried ambushing me at Sal's.

Justin's bungalow was in the northern suburbs and looked dark and deserted. It was a white house with black trim, much smaller than most of the others on the block, but kept up very well. There was a metal fence around the front yard and I began to consider the possibility that he might have a dog. I reached into my purse and pulled out a small can of pepper spray that I also carried around with me. I didn't like the thought of using it on any animal, but I wasn't about to die because of one. A guy like Tank could have a slew of Pitbulls strutting around his place, and with my luck, they'd get me before he ever could.

I hurried across the dark street and made it over the sidewalk, up the lawn, and to the back of the house, my heart beating loudly. Trying not to make any noise, I unlatched the metal gate and crept into the backyard, which was relatively private. Behind the house was a large garage, with an alley. I decided that if I made it out of this situation alive, I'd try to escape that way.

Looking back at the house, I released a shaky breath, stepped onto the low deck, which wrapped around the back of the house, and quietly made my way to the patio door. Glancing inside, I saw, nor heard any evidence of a pet and pulled on the door handle. When it slid open, I couldn't believe it. Either I had the wrong house or my luck was starting to turn around. Hoping for the change of luck, I quietly let myself in.

THIRTEEN

TANK

ERA CALLED ME back when I was about two blocks from my home and gave me the most recent address on file for Raina Davis. I pulled over to the side of the road and wrote it down.

"So, now that I've scratched your back, when you going to return the favor?" she asked, a smile in her voice.

"Do you have something in mind?"

"To be honest, I need some help with my mother's car. It won't start and I've been driving her ass everywhere. Neither of us have the money right now to get it checked out. Could you stop by and take a look at it?"

"Of course," I replied. "I can look at it in the next couple of days. Let me call you tomorrow and we'll figure something out."

"Thanks, Tank," she said. "I really appreciate it."

"No problem. You don't want to get together, later tonight, do you?"

"I have to work early. Otherwise, you know I'd love to see you."

"I understand. I appreciate you getting the address for me, though."

"What exactly do you need it for?"

"I'm looking for someone that she knows."

Vera didn't say anything.

"It's really no big deal," I added. "I've been trying to find her friend, and this will make it easier."

"So, Raina is not in any kind of trouble with you guys?"

"Not that I'm aware of. I just need to speak to her."

She sighed. "Good. I don't want to get into any trouble."

"As far as I'm concerned, we never had this conversation."

"Yeah, same with me."

"I'll call you in the morning, around nine?"

"Sure. Sounds good. I'll call Mom and let her know what's up."

"You do that. Bye, Vera. Thanks again."

"You're welcome."

We hung up and I turned the car around. Raina's apartment building wasn't too far from Raptor's old place and I was only minutes away. When I arrived at the complex, I recognized the building. I'd been there before, buying coke, just a week ago. The memory made me anxious and suddenly in need of a line.

"Fuck," I muttered, trying not to give in to the craving. I knew it would be easy to call the dealer and set up a pickup. But, I'd made a promise to Bastard about keeping my shit together, and the thought of cornering Raina was almost a high in itself.

Not as high as it would be with a couple of harmless snorts of coke...

Trying to ignore the devil in my head, I parked the car and jogged up to the complex, which was secure. Fortunately, two women were leaving the building and I caught the door.

"Thanks," I said, smiling at them.

The two looked at each other and I could tell by their expressions that they weren't sure if they should have let me in.

"Do you live here?" asked one of them, a skinny redhead with glasses.

Shit.

Not needing a scene, I made up a story. "No. Don't say anything, but I'm the surprise stripper for a bachelorette party in this building."

They both smiled.

"Sorry, we don't know of any bachelorette party," said the other one, a short brunette. "Otherwise, we'd love to see you strut your stuff. And something tells me that your show," her eyes went to my zipper, "is very big."

I smiled. "I can hold my own."

"I bet you can," she purred.

"I've never seen a male stripper perform before," said the redhead, staring at my bicep. "Can I just feel your arm for a second?"

I flexed both of them. "Have at it."

She touched the muscle in my left arm and sighed in pleasure. "You must work out a lot."

"About an hour a day, give or take," I replied.

"It certainly shows," she said, removing her hand. "You're ripped."

"Thank you."

"We'd better let him get to that party, Bonnie," said the brunette, pulling her away. "Before the bride gets too drunk."

"Goodbye," said Bonnie. "Hope you pull in a lot of money tonight."

"Thanks," I said, watching them get into a Ford Focus. The redhead blew me a kiss. I waved and then proceeded to find Raina's apartment, which was on the third floor. Upon reaching it, I pulled my gun out, knocked on the door, and waited. When she didn't answer, I pulled out the small tool kit from my back pocket, and quickly jimmied the lock.

The first thing I noticed, upon entering the apartment, was a pair of boy's small tennis shoes sitting by the door and I wondered if Vera's information had been wrong. I hadn't heard anything about Raina having children.

Keeping the light off, I began searching the place for clues as to who really did live there. One thing I noticed was that someone liked fairies, scented candles, and books. Not only did I almost knock over several figurines, but there was a stack of romance novels sitting next to the sofa, that almost had me doing a face-plant. Muttering to myself, I continued my search and walked down the hallway to check out the bedrooms. The smallest of the two had blue curtains, a toddler bed, with a Choo-Choo train comforter, and a wall decal which read 'Billy'. There was also a toy box and a small rocking chair next to a bookshelf.

Dammit, I thought, now thinking that I indeed had the wrong apartment.

Frustrated, I walked into the other bedroom and paused when I saw the mess. There were clothes strewn all over, an old pizza box about ready to fall off of the nightstand, and two empty bottles of wine lying on the floor next to the bed. Frowning, I stepped closer to the nightstand and found a picture of a young boy with dark blonde curls. He also had a cute smile and eyes that reminded me of Raina's. The child had to be hers.

I left the bedroom and began searching the kitchen and living room for information on Cole, such as an address or even a picture. Fortunately, I lucked out and found an old card envelope with an address in Davenport. Hoping he still lived there, I shoved it into my pocket and made my way to the door. I didn't feel like confronting her anymore. Not here at her place, especially if there was a kid involved.

As I walked through the living room, something caught my eye on the coffee table.

An urn.

I picked it up and read the inscription etched on the vase. Although I'd never met him, my heart clenched when I realized whose ashes were inside – Billy's. The child had only been two years old. When I read the date of his death, it made the hair stand up on the back of my neck. He'd died the day before my old man had been murdered. I didn't know if it meant anything, but it sure seemed like a hell of a coincidence.

Rubbing my hand over my face, I decided to wait around for a couple of hours to see if she showed up. I needed to talk to her and find out what happened to Billy. I wasn't even sure why it was so important to me, but something in my gut told me it was. I sat down on the sofa and stared at the urn. Losing my father had been hard. He'd been everything to me. But even I knew that there was nothing like losing a child, especially one so young. She'd mentioned that her life was a mess and now I understood to what extent. The kind of grief that Raina was going through had to be tough.

My phone buzzed and I noticed it was a text message from Raptor asking how things were going. I explained that Raina wasn't home and that I'd be keeping watch for a couple of hours. I then told him to go home to Adriana and that I'd get back to him when I learned anything new. Afterward, I put my phone away and sat alone in the darkness, waiting for answers.

FOURTEEN

RAINA

JUSTIN'S HOUSE WAS spacious and relatively clean. His upstairs furniture had seen better days, but the basement below looked like it had been recently remodeled. Not only did it contain an expansive bar, a television that was obnoxiously huge, and two pinball machines, but there was a leather sectional that looked like it cost more than all of my furniture combined. Not to mention his pool table, the workout area, and another room with a hot tub. It was definitely a bachelor pad.

Muttering to myself about dirty money, I walked back to the main floor of the house and sat down on the sofa, which faced the driveway. It was getting late and I wasn't sure what time Tank might arrive home, but it didn't matter. Now that his old man had killed my child, I had nothing better to do with my time than to wait to return the favor.

FIFTEEN

TANK

AFTER WAITING AROUND for a couple of hours, I began to wonder if she might have skipped town and if I was just wasting my time. Eventually, I nodded off until the sound of keys in the front door jolted me awake. Jumping to my feet, I took out the gun, and moved into the hallway just as the door opened.

"Raina?" called a man's voice.

I stepped around the corner. "She isn't here," I said, recognizing the stranger. He was the owner of Sal's. We'd never formally met, but I'd seen him around town.

Sal, shocked, took a step back. "What in the hell are you doing here?"

"Looking for Raina. What are you doing here?" I asked, frowning.

"Looking for her, too. She's my niece."

My eyes widened. "Your niece?" I repeated.

He nodded, his eyes on my gun. "Yes. What do you want with her?"

"It's club business."

His lips thinned. "Club business? Now, look... I'm not sure what kind of *business* you have with her, but she's a good girl."

"I'm sure you're right," I said. "Her brother, on the other hand, is in deep shit."

He heaved a heavy sigh. "Dammit, I was afraid you were going to say that. What has he gotten himself into?"

"Something he shouldn't have. Do you know who I am?"

"Yeah. You're a member of the Gold Vipers."

"I'm their newest president."

"Congratulations," he said dryly.

My eye twitched. "There's nothing to celebrate. I'm only the president because someone killed my old man, who held the position before me. Your nephew knows who the shooter is."

He sighed. "I'm sorry for your loss. I met Slammer a couple of times and he seemed like a good guy."

"He was, unlike the pieces of shit that Cole is involved with."

"I won't argue that. Look, why aren't you hassling him instead of sneaking into Raina's house? She's been through enough and doesn't need to be involved with this."

"I tried talking to Raina about this civilly," I lied, "but she bailed on me, which leads me to believe that your niece knows something useful. All I want to know is where Cole is, so I can find out who murdered my father."

"Why don't you let the police figure that out?"

"Because I want to handle this my way," I said, getting frustrated. I was tired, hungry, and not in the mood for conversation. At least not with this guy. "Enough with the questions. Tell me where Cole is and I'll get out of your hair."

"I have no idea, and the truth is, I wouldn't tell you if I knew," he said evenly.

Clenching my teeth, I cocked the gun. "Don't fuck with me, old man. This is some serious shit."

He leaned forward, a stubborn look on his face. "And I'm serious when I say that you won't be getting any information from me."

"You prepared to die because of it?" I asked, trying not to explode. I wasn't about to kill Sal, but he was seriously pissing me off.

"Son, I'm dying anyway," he said with a grim smile. "Hell, you may as well just put a bullet through my head and save me from racking up thousands of dollars in medical expenses. I'd rather not put my family through that anyway."

"You're dying?" I asked. I had to admit, he wasn't the picture of good health.

"It's my liver." He raised his left hand, which was shaking. "In fact, I could really use a fucking drink right now. Just to take the edge off."

Seeing the truth in his eyes, I uncocked the gun and put it away. "Looks like the last thing you need is a drink, Sal."

Relaxing, he slowly headed toward the kitchen. "You've never walked in my shoes, so don't go presuming what I need."

"No, and you've never walked in mine either. If you had you'd understand why I'm so fucking upset."

Sal reached up into one of the cupboards and pulled out a bottle of whiskey. "Look, I understand your anger, but there's no sense in committing any more violence or murder. It's only going to promote more of it, and in the long run, nobody wins."

Spying a box of toothpicks next to the stove, I walked over and grabbed one. I needed a cigarette. Badly. "If I wanted a preacher, I'd go to church. What I need is your nephew's address."

He poured himself a small shot-glass of whiskey and stared at it with a frown. "All I know is that he's out of town."

"I already know that. Where out of town?"

Sal picked up the whiskey, his hand trembling. "I'm not too sure," he replied, before slamming it down.

"Better?" I asked dryly.

"You have no idea."

Licking my lips, I resisted an urge to pour one myself. "Raina know you have liver disease?"

He wiped his mouth and turned back to me. "Pretty much. I told her I was waiting for my test results."

"You get them yet?"

Sal shook his head. "No. But I know what it's going to say."

"Then why are you still drinking?" I asked, nodding toward the bottle.

"Guess you and I aren't so different when it comes to living dangerously," he said with a funny smile.

"Maybe not," I replied, thinking of my own many vices.

We were both silent for a few moments. Then he looked at me again. "Tell you what, I'll call him and see what he knows."

I grunted. "I highly doubt he'd give up the information that easily and that's why I need to talk to him face-to-face."

"I know why you need to speak to him *face-to-face* –

you're planning on roughing him up."

"Not if he gives me what I need."

Sal scowled at me. "I'm not going to set that up. Now look, I know he's made some mistakes, but he's not a killer."

"He wasn't the one who pulled the trigger. Rumor has it the shooter was female."

His eyebrows shot up. "A woman?"

"That's what I hear."

Sal poured himself another shot. "So, some woman shot your old man. Did he do her wrong? Break her heart or beat her up?"

"No. He was happily married and wasn't into beating chicks."

He smirked. "Right. I've heard how you bikers treat women."

"Don't be an asshole. A man doesn't have to be a biker to beat up a woman. Just a pussy. So, quit stereotyping," I said angrily.

He mumbled something under his breath.

My fist grew itchy, but I ignored it. He was an old, dying man and even I wasn't that much of a prick. "We already know that the Devil's Rangers set it up," I said, changing the subject.

"What for? A payback?"

"You ask a lot of questions."

"If you want my help, you'd better answer them," he said, looking a lot more courageous than before the booze.

"The Devil's Rangers are responsible for a lot of innocent lives, including Slammer's and my girlfriend's," I answered coldly. "Now, I'm through with your questions. I need answers myself."

"Your girlfriend was murdered by that club?" he asked, looking taken aback.

"Yes. She was young and innocent, too. They did it just to prove a point."

He poured himself another shot. "I guess I can see why you're pissed off. If Cole knew they killed a young woman for spite, he wouldn't want anything to do with them. One thing I know is that he has ethics, despite his affiliation with that damn club."

"Ethics, huh? Then let me talk to him so I can get the answers I need."

He drank the shot and slammed the glass onto the counter. "Tell me something – what are you going to do when you get ahold of this woman who supposedly shot Slammer? Kill her?"

"To be perfectly honest, as much as I'd *like* to kill the bitch, I'm going to make sure that the person who ordered the hit is the one that pays."

He put the bottle of whiskey back into the cupboard and then reached into his pocket. Sal pulled out a pen and removed the cap. "You have a phone number where I can reach you?"

I let out a sigh. "Sure." I gave it to him and watched as he wrote it down on a paper napkin.

"Now, get out of my niece's apartment, and when I find out who's responsible for Slammer's death, I'll call you."

"You think you can find out, just like that?" I asked, smirking.

"I own a damn bar. I've got plenty of contacts who can find these things out for me. I also have a lot of favors that need to be returned. I'm going to start calling on them."

I stared at Sal. If I let him leave without getting the information I'd come for, I might not ever see Raina or Cole again. He'd most definitely call and warn them. "Why should I trust you?"

"Because as much as I know my life is over, I want my sister's kids to live on. I know all about your club and what you're capable of."

I smiled coldly. "No, you don't know what we're capable of and that's why you'd better not fuck me over."

"Don't worry. I won't," he replied, swaying slightly.

"Fine then. Since you're hell-bent on drinking yourself to death, make sure you get me the info before you get that far."

He grunted. "I'll do my best."

"Just do it," I snapped before leaving the apartment.

SIXTEEN

RAINA

I T WAS SHORTLY after two a.m. when I saw a black pickup truck pull into the driveway. Frightened, but determined to confront Justin, I bent down and watched from the window as he shut off the lights and headed toward the house carrying a bag of fast food. When I heard the key turn in the deadbolt, I hid inside the pantry and waited as he entered the house, whistling.

Trying not to lose my courage, I listened as he made his way through the living room and into the kitchen. Taking a deep breath, I raised my gun and stepped out. He had his back to me and was searching in the refrigerator for something.

"Would you like a bite to eat?" he asked in an amused voice. "I ordered a lot of food."

My heart skipped a beat. "How did you know I was here?"

"Your perfume. I recognized it the moment I entered the living room," he said, closing the refrigerator. He walked over to the counter and began pulling out food from the bags. The smell of bacon and French fries made my stomach growl.

"I didn't put any perfume on today."

Justin unwrapped one of the burgers and licked some ketchup from his finger. "Then it must be your shampoo or something. Whatever it is, it gave you away. Next time you'll know to be more careful." He grabbed a French fry and shoved it into his mouth.

Hating the mocking tone, I cocked the gun. "Let go of the food, raise your hands in the air."

"But, I'm hungry, and believe me, you won't like me when I'm hungry."

"I don't like you now."

"I'm definitely feeling that vibe, Princess," he replied, a smile in his voice.

"Call me that again and the only thing you'll be feeling is a coffin. Now get your fucking hands in the air!"

Sighing, he did what I asked.

"Now, sit down," I said, nodding toward kitchen table.

"Can I bring my food?"

I stared at him incredulously. I was threatening him with a gun and all he could think about was eating. "Seriously?"

"Of course I'm serious. It's been hours since I've eaten and my food is going to get cold and mushy. I didn't pay twenty dollars to see all of it go to waste."

"Oh, well then by all means, don't let me stop you from stuffing your face."

"You want a burger?" he said, ignoring my sarcasm. "I have an extra double-cheeseburger with bacon and the works, if you want it."

"I don't want anything."

"Suit yourself." He grabbed the food and brought it to the kitchen table where he sat down. "To be honest, I'm glad you're here, although I don't know how you made it inside. I had extra locks put on all of my doors."

"Your patio slider was unlocked."

He sighed. "Dammit."

"You of all people should know to be more careful," I said dryly. "Prez."

He unfolded one of the burgers, which was dripping with grease.

"I guess I should. My mind had been on other shit lately."

"What do you mean, *you're glad I'm here*?" I asked, ignoring his comment.

Not answering, he stood back up.

"What are you doing?" I asked.

"Getting something to drink. You want a beer?"

"No," I said, watching as he opened up the refrigerator again and pulled out a bottle of light beer. He untwisted the top and took a long swig, then went back over to the table and sat back down.

"Are you going to answer my question, or what?" I asked, getting angrier by the minute. Obviously, he wasn't at all concerned with my presence.

"Oh. Yeah, sorry. We needed to talk. That's why I'm glad you're here. I'm just wondering why you came to me."

"I'm sure it's obvious."

He grunted. "Obvious? No. Nothing a woman does is 'obvious'."

"I might not be obvious but you're certainly typical."

Justin scowled. "What is that supposed to mean?"

"Isn't it *obvious*?" I said, sarcasm dripping from my tongue. "You're a chauvinistic pig. I guess that seems to be pretty 'typical' of guys like you who hang out in biker gangs."

"I'm not in a biker gang. I belong to a motorcycle club."

I rolled my eyes. "Funny how you're only really correcting me on the latter part of my statement."

His eyes glittered. "I'll be the first to admit, I think women are at their best in the bedroom, in the kitchen –"

I shook my head. "You're truly an asshole."

He raised his hand. "You didn't let me finish. I was going to add that you're also great in the laundry room, the grocery store, and… oh yeah. Restaurants. You don't see very many guys changing diapers in the men's room."

"Unbelievable."

Justin laughed. "You can't honestly think that I'd admit to feeling that way if I really did?"

I rubbed my temple. "What I'm thinking right now is that I should just shoot you in the mouth so you'll stop running it."

"Is that why you're here? To shoot me?"

"Maybe."

"No. I don't think so." His face became serious as he studied mine. "If you wanted me dead, you'd have done it by now."

I wasn't sure what I wanted anymore. "Why were you at Sal's tonight?" I asked, changing the subject.

"I was looking for you," he said, biting into his burger.

"And you found me. I guess it's good that I didn't accept that date from you. I'd probably be dead by now."

He finished chewing and answered. "I'm not interested in killing you."

Right, I thought. "What do you want from me?"

"Information. I need to know where your brother, Cole, is."

My eyes widened. "My brother? Why?"

"He can lead me to the person who killed my old man. Did he tell you anything about the shooter?"

My heart pounded loudly in my chest. I was sure he could hear it. "I… no. He didn't."

"Look, because I like you and Sal has enough shit to worry about, I'll let Cole live if he gives up the name of the shooter. So call him or give me an address for the little shit."

He didn't know it was me. Otherwise, I'd be dead right now.

"Sal has enough shit to worry about?" I repeated. "What do you know about Sal's problems?"

"I ran into him tonight. He mentioned a few things during the conversation."

"I didn't know you were friends."

"We aren't. So, are you going to answer my question? Where's your brother?"

I let out a ragged breath. It was time to get this over with. "You don't need Cole to tell you who killed Slammer."

His eyes narrowed. "You know who it was?"

Before I could confess and let him know why I'd killed his old man, we heard the rumble of several motorcycles approaching.

Fuck!

"You expecting someone?"

"No, but that doesn't mean anything," he said, standing up. "My brothers are always showing up all hours of the night."

I backed toward the door leading to the living room. I needed to get out of there.

"Relax and put the gun down. Nobody has to know that you were here threatening me."

As I was about to answer, gunfire broke out in front of the house. Swearing, Justin flew toward me and the next thing I knew, we were on the ground, his body covering mine.

"Stay down," he ordered, grabbing the gun out of my hand with little effort.

More shots. This time, through the wall above us.

"Fucking assholes," he growled next to my ear as the sound of motorcycles faded into the distance.

"Are they leaving?"

"I don't know."

"Who do you think they were?"

"Probably the Devil's Rangers."

"Oh." For some reason, I felt oddly comforted by that knowledge and wondered if Cole had called them.

We heard voices outside.

"Oh, my God," I whispered, suddenly terrified.

"Get under the table," he whispered, pushing me toward it.

I crawled underneath and turned to watch him get into a crouched position. "What are you going to do?"

"Beat someone's ass if I get the chance," he replied, pulling another gun from an ankle holster. "Don't leave the kitchen."

"Wait. Give me my gun," I said, holding out my hand.

Justin hesitated. "Just don't aim the damn thing at me, woman," he replied, handing it to me.

"Don't do anything that will make me want to aim it at you, *mister*," I replied, grabbing it from him.

Smirking, he slipped out of the kitchen.

Trying to remain calm, I let out a shaky breath and then waited for several seconds before attempting to make my own escape. When I thought it might be safe, I scooted out from under the table and stood up, still half expecting to be shot through the wall. Saying a prayer, I walked toward the back door of the house just as police sirens began to blare in the distance.

"It was actually the neighbors we heard talking outside. They called the cops," said Justin from behind me.

I turned around quickly. "Did anyone get hurt?"

"No, but I've got a few windows to replace, including the ones in my truck. When I find out who did this, believe me, someone will get hurt."

"Did anyone see who they were?"

"One of my neighbors, Will, said he couldn't see the patches clearly, but it was definitely a motorcycle club. I'm sure it was the Devil's Rangers. They're the only ones who do this kind of shit."

"Really?" I sneered, unable to believe the shit he was flinging. "Your crew doesn't do drive-bys?"

"Hell no," he replied, looking disgusted. "We usually stand and fight our enemies. Face-to-face. Drive-bys are for pussies."

The blood rushed to my head. "Cole said your club was responsible for the one in Davenport a couple weeks ago. A party that the Devil's Rangers had hosted."

"Yeah, well he's wrong. Sure, they tried pinning that on us, but, it's not how we operate. Believe me, they know it wasn't us, either."

A cold fist seemed to close around my heart. I began to break out in a cold sweat as the impact of what he was saying really started to sink in.

"Are you okay? You look like you're going to faint," Justin remarked. The concern on his face made everything that much worse. The man seemed genuinely worried and had no idea of what I'd done.

"I'm fine. I have to go," I said, my voice hoarse.

"At least wait until the cops leave," he replied as the doorbell rang. "They have it out for me and I could use a witness."

"Sure." It was the least that I could do. Everything was my fault. *Everything.* Unless he was putting me on? But, why would he? "Can I use your bathroom?" I asked as he began to walk away.

Justin half-turned and waved his thumb. "Yeah. It's the first door on the left."

I rushed inside and barely made it to the toilet before I threw up.

SEVENTEEN

TANK

RAINA WAS QUIET and unusually pale when the police asked us questions about the shootings.

"No, I have no idea who shot at my house," I told them, wanting to handle the matter myself.

"Is that right?" answered one of the cops, Mike Tolbert, with a cool smile. "It's funny how you're drawing a complete blank. As usual..."

"I'm sorry, have we met?" I asked, glaring at the man. His attitude pissed me off and I was already in a pissy mood. "Because you seem to think you know a lot about me when I've never seen you before in my life. Hell, maybe you know something about tonight's shooting?"

"You and I both know that it has something to do with club rivalry. If you don't want to do any follow-up on this, or press charges, that's your right, but don't think for a second that if someone from the Devil's Rangers goes missing or turns up dead, we won't be back," answered Tolbert.

"Suit yourself, but I've got no beef with the Devil's Rangers," I lied.

The two cops looked at each other.

"He's right," said Raina. "My brother is part of that club and it's all good."

Grateful that she was helping, I hid my surprise. "See, I told you. Everything is all warm and fuzzy between us now."

"Right," said the other cop, Bill Shaw. "Well, then. I guess since we have both of your statements, our business is done here."

"I agree," I said, opening the door for them. "Have a good night."

"You too, Mr. Fleming," said Shaw, walking outside.

"Let us know if you remember anything about the shooters,"

said Tolbert, talking to Raina.

"I didn't see them," she replied.

"Okay, if you *heard* anything besides the sound of their engines. A voice or anything that could help," Tolbert said in a condescending tone. Like she was just some bubble-head.

"Oh, don't worry. You'll be the first person I'll call," she said tightly.

Tolbert looked at me. "We'll be watching you and the rest of your gang."

"Funny, I was just a victim of a drive-by and you're treating me like a felon," I said with a cold smile.

"Don't act like you're some kind of saint. This wasn't a random act and nobody else in the neighborhood had their windows blown out. You're on somebody's shit list and now they're back on yours. I should just arrest you now before you order a hit on the people who did this, *Prez.*"

"More assumptions," I said sharply. "Instead of giving me the third degree, maybe you should be out looking for the guys who did this."

"We all know who did this but you don't want to press charges. Isn't that right, Mr. Fleming?"

"Even if I knew, I sure as hell wouldn't have called you."

"You didn't call us anyway," he replied.

"Why would I when you treat victims like criminals?"

He looked at Raina. "Don't let him fool you, Miss. This guy isn't just a criminal, he's a murderer. You should really keep better company."

"If Justin is a criminal, why hasn't *he* been arrested?" she asked, crossing her arms under her chest.

"Because he's full of shit. I should sue you for slander," replied Justin before Tolbert could answer.

"Go ahead. See where that gets you," replied the cop. He looked back at Raina. "I'm not trying to upset you. Just looking out for your best interests, Miss Davis."

She nodded curtly.

"You too, Mr. Fleming. I'm sure we'll be seeing each other real soon."

I didn't answer him.

Mumbling something under his breath, he left, closing the door behind him.

"I have to go," said Raina, quickly.

"Not yet. We still haven't some unfinished business," I said, taking out my phone.

"Please. I shouldn't have come here. It was a mistake."

"What was?" I asked, texting Raptor about what had happened.

"To ask that you leave Cole alone."

I looked up from my phone. "I will if he gives me the name of the shooter. I already told you that."

"And…what are you going to do when you find out who did it?" she asked, looking pale again.

"It's not your concern."

"Are you going to kill her?"

"Probably not. I have bigger fish to fry, and unlike your brother's club, we don't kill women. Call him. Please. Try and talk some sense into the kid."

Sighing, Raina pulled out her own phone and turned it on.

"You turned your phone off?"

"Yes. I didn't want to be disturbed. Good thing, too, because I missed a few calls. Speaking of which…" she said, just as her phone began to ring.

"Who is it? Your brother?"

"No. It's my sister-in-law, Joanna. It must be important if she's calling in the middle of the night."

I sighed.

Raina answered the phone and it was obvious from the conversation they were having that the woman on the other end was both excited and upset. Raina tried calming her down but then a look of shock flashed across her face.

EIGHTTEEN

RAINA

"WHAT... WHAT DID you just say?" I asked Joanna, who wasn't making any sense.

"I saw Billy. He's alive," she repeated and then gasped. "Oh, my God. It's Phillip. He's home. He must have seen me."

Stunned that I'd heard her right, my heart began to pound. "Wait. What do you mean that Billy is alive?"

"Phillip was at the cabin. I thought he was cheating on me, so I drove up there. I peeked into the window and saw him up there, with your son," she whispered quickly.

"That's impossible," I said in a husky voice. I'd seen my son's lifeless body in the hospital before they'd wheeled him away. His ashes were now in the urn, sitting in my living room.

"I know but... I also know what I saw. I have to go. He's hollering for me." Joanna hung up.

I slipped the phone into my purse, my mind still trying to wrap around what she'd just told me. My level-headed, successful, lawyer sister-in-law had just claimed that she'd seen my son *alive*. It sounded crazy but I could tell from her voice that whatever she'd seen had rattled the hell out of her.

"What's going on?" asked Justin.

I forced a smile. "I don't know. I think my sister-in-law is losing her mind."

"You asked her about Billy. Was that your son?"

"Yes," I said, feeling suddenly exhausted.

"What happened to him?" Justin asked softly.

"He was killed."

His eyes widened in surprise. "What do you mean?"

"There was this party and... the gal who was supposed to be watching Billy dragged him to it. There was some shooting involved and he... he was hit."

Justin grabbed my hand. "I'm so sorry for your loss, Raina. I can't imagine the shit you've been going through."

"It hasn't been easy," I admitted, unable to look him in the eye. "I know it hasn't been for you either. With your father being killed."

"No, but your son was so young. He had his entire life ahead of him."

All I could do was nod.

"I take it you're talking about the Devil's Rangers' party?"

"Yes."

"Listen to me," he said, tipping my chin back so he could look into my eyes. "My club had nothing to do with that. I swear to God."

"Cole said it *was* your guys. That you were retaliating for some other things that went on before."

"Cole is either lying or was highly misinformed. Like I told you before, we don't do that shit. Slammer would have never ordered something like that. Neither would I. When we have a problem with someone, we look them in the eye and take care of business. Whoever was responsible for the shooting that night wasn't a Gold Viper. I give you my word."

I believed him and the shame that I felt for killing his father made me sick. "I believe you," I said, trying to prepare myself for the confession that I was about to do. I owed it to Justin, and no matter what happened, I was prepared to face the consequences. Even if it meant going to prison or... death.

"Good."

"There's something you should know," I said, letting out a ragged breath.

His eyes bore into mine. "I already do. It's pretty obvious."

I could barely breathe as we sat there staring at each other. I could tell from his expression that we were talking about the same thing.

After a few more seconds, I had to break the silence. I needed to know what he was going to do to me. "Are you going to have me arrested?"

"I'm not sure."

"I'm... so sorry. I... thought that he –"

"No. You were *told* that my father ordered the shooting that killed your son," he interrupted. "You needed to hurt the man responsible. I may hate what you did. But, I do understand why you wanted revenge."

"You do?" I asked, somewhat relieved. There was a sadness in his eyes that made my heart heavy, however.

He nodded. "I probably would have done the same thing."

"I'm so sorry," I said, reaching out to him.

He raised a hand between us, stopping me from touching him. "Just because I get it, doesn't mean we're friends. I need you to leave."

"Yes. Of course," I replied, taking a step back just as my phone began to ring. I looked down and saw that it was Cole. I ignored it.

Justin was silent as I grabbed my purse and headed to the doorway. Before I walked out, however, he asked me what Joanna had said about Billy.

I turned around. "She claimed to have seen him at their cabin."

"Is it even possible?"

"No. The last time I saw my son he was clearly dead," I replied.

He nodded and said nothing more.

I closed the door behind me and left.

NINETEEN

TANK

"**W**HAT EXACTLY HAPPENED?" asked Raptor, calling me a few minutes later.

I told him everything, including Raina's admittance of killing my father.

"So, her son was shot and she blamed Slammer?"

I pulled out a pack of cigarettes from the freezer. "It sounds like she was told that he ordered the drive-by. The Devil's Rangers pinned it on him."

Raptor let out a heavy sigh. "Now they're shooting up your place. I'd better warn the others."

"Yeah, you'd better. Although, I think it was more of a warning from the Devil's Rangers, by Cole's request." I lit a cigarette and took a deep drag. "I'm sure they had no idea Raina was in my house."

"Maybe, but we can't take any chances."

"I know. We need to call a meeting tomorrow and let everyone know what's going on."

"Good idea. What about the girl? Raina?"

I thought about the pain, grief, and guilt she was now feeling. I could tell that she'd been remorseful about killing my father. She'd been through enough. "Nothing."

"What about having her arrested?"

"Hell no. She's already living in her own prison," I said, thinking back to her apartment, especially her son's bedroom. "We both lost people we loved and can't bring them back. I'm not going to hurt her or send her to jail. We let it rest."

"Sure. What about tonight's shooters?"

"We catch those fuckers and take them down."

"Okay."

I yawned. "I'm bushed. Let's plan on meeting later this evening. Around seven."

He agreed and we hung up. I cleaned up the glass and left a message for a guy I knew that replaced windows. Afterward, I fell asleep on the sofa, my gun close.

TWENTY

RAINA

I FELT EMPTY INSIDE when I left Justin's place. Part of me was relieved that he'd let me walk out the door, another part wanted to be punished for killing his father.

As I got into my car, my phone rang. It was Cole.

"Where have you been?" he barked. "Sal and I have been trying to call you for the last couple of hours."

"I've been busy. Cole, who in the hell told you that the Gold Vipers were responsible for the drive-by that killed Billy?" I asked sharply.

"Ronnie," he replied. "He's our V.P. Why? What's the problem?"

"Because he was wrong and I killed an innocent man," I snapped.

"Hold on a minute. Why would you say that?"

"I just left Tank's place and there is no way the Gold Vipers were responsible for the drive-by."

"What? You were actually there? Are you fucking crazy?"

"Honestly, I feel crazy right now. But even more than that, I feel like a cold-blooded murderer," I said, rubbing the bridge of my nose.

"What brought all of this on?"

"We had a long conversation and he told me that they are against drive-bys."

"And you believe him?" he asked dryly.

"Yes I do. Cole, I admitted to killing his father and he let me walk out of his house alive."

He gasped. "You told him the truth?"

"I had to, Cole. I owed it to him," I said, staring out into the darkness.

"What is wrong with you? Are you on some kind of suicide mission?" he asked angrily. "I mean what in the hell were you thinking, going over there?"

"I needed to confront him."

"Why? You knew he was looking for you."

"Yes, and I wasn't about to go into hiding for the rest of my life. Anyway, I'm glad I did. Now we both know the truth."

"This is insane."

"What is insane is that I almost died tonight because of the drive-by *your* club orchestrated."

"I don't know anything about a drive-by tonight. But I do know that Ronnie wouldn't lie to me about who killed Billy. It was the Gold Vipers."

I still didn't buy it. "Then why didn't Justin kill me?"

"Justin?"

"Tank," I huffed, "or whatever the hell they call him. Listen to me, you were fed the wrong information and now... I have to live with killing an innocent man."

"My club wouldn't lie to me."

"They aren't your club, Cole. Not yet. You're just a damn prospect which, as far as I'm concerned, is high-minded."

"You really told him that you killed his father, the leader of the Gold Vipers, and he let you walk away?" he asked, ignoring my snide comment.

"You're talking to me, aren't you? He should have put a bullet through my head," I said miserably. "Like I did to Slammer. He owed me that much."

"What did he say when you confessed?"

I went over the conversation.

"Is he still looking for me?"

"I don't think so but he's going to go after the Devil's Rangers for shooting up his house. You can count on that."

"Fuck. Listen, I don't know what the hell is going on. If there was a drive-by tonight, I wasn't told about it."

"But, you're a prospect. I'm sure they don't tell you everything."

"I need to talk to Ronnie. He'll want to know about this."

"Dammit, Cole. What you need to do is get the hell away from that club before you get yourself killed."

"Don't worry about me, Raina," he replied. "I'll be fine."

"Cole –"

"I'll call you later," he said and then hung up before I could say anything more.

Swearing, I threw the phone on the passenger seat and drove home.

IT WAS JUST after three a.m. by the time I made it home. I left a message for Sal, letting him know that I was fine and would call him later in the day. Afterward, I ate a piece of bread and peanut butter, and then crashed from exhaustion. When my alarm went off at eleven a.m., it took everything I had to drag myself out of bed and into the shower. But, I'd made a decision before falling asleep, and was determined to follow through with it. Sometime today I planned on turning myself into the police for the murder of Justin's father,

Slammer. If I didn't, I knew I could never live with myself.

When I was finished with my shower, I slipped on the black dress that I'd worn to my son's funeral, and put my hair up into a bun. As I was searching for my black pumps, I heard my cell phone go off.

"Hello?" I said, not recognizing the phone number.

"Hi, Raina. It's Phillip," said my brother-in-law.

"Oh. Hi. I didn't recognize the number."

"I'm calling from the hospital."

Mark's older brother, Phillip, was a surgeon at St. Luke's Hospital, which was only a few miles away. We'd always had a strained relationship, mostly because he had never approved of me and I'd always thought him to be an arrogant, stuffy bastard. After Mark had died, he'd warmed up slightly, at least in front of others. I still felt uncomfortable talking with him, though. "I see. How have you been?"

"Good. How about yourself?"

"Oh. You know... I'm getting by."

"It will get easier. It just takes time," he replied, as if talking about the weather.

"That's what I hear."

"The reason I'm calling is because I noticed that Joanna contacted you late last night."

"Yes," I replied.

"What did she want?"

"She just called to see how I was doing. Why?" I lied. Although I knew there was no possible way that she could have seen Billy alive, something seemed off.

He let out a ragged sigh. "Joanna had a nervous breakdown early this morning. She tried killing herself."

My eyes widened. "She did?"

"Yes," he replied, sounding torn up. "She tried overdosing on some sleeping pills. Luckily, I found her in the bathroom, with the bottle, and stopped her from taking a handful of them."

"Oh, my God. She's okay, though, right?"

"Physically, yes. Mentally, she's going through a tough time. I actually have someone staying with her today, while I'm at the hospital. I'm afraid she'll try it again."

"Do you know why she would do something like that?" I asked. The Joanna that I knew had always seemed so happy. Although, she certainly hadn't sounded like herself on the phone earlier.

"Honestly, I don't know what's going on with her. First, she tried accusing me of cheating and then she came up with some cockamamie story about Billy."

"What story was that?" I asked, not wanting to admit that I already knew.

"For some crazy reason, she thinks that he's alive. I know it's crazy and I probably shouldn't even be bothering you with this nonsense, but I wanted to find out if she said anything to you. I'd hate to think she upset you with such a tale."

"I'm fine," I said. "I'm more worried about Joanna. This doesn't sound like her at all. Is she on some kind of medication?"

"No. I think Billy's death might have hit her hard, too. I'm not sure if you knew, but she couldn't have children. It's been very troubling for her, especially the last couple of years."

"I had no idea. I'm sorry." I'd always figured that they just didn't want children. They were extremely wealthy and lived very busy lives.

"We were planning on adopting, but I don't know now. The fact that she tried taking her life…" his voice trailed off, and for the first time, I felt some real emotion coming from him.

"Maybe Billy's death has taken a harder toll on her than you thought," I replied. I knew Joanna and Phillip had adored Billy. They would always lavish him with gifts on Christmas and his birthday.

"Maybe. Anyway, I just don't want her upsetting you with crazy stories."

"I'm not upset. Don't worry."

"That's a relief. I've been thinking – maybe you could come over and join us for dinner soon. I think it will help Joanna a little. When you're feeling up to it, that is."

"Sure," I replied, not up to telling him about my plans for the day.

"Definitely." He swore. "I'm being paged. I've got to go."

"No problem. Goodbye, Phillip. Tell Joanna I'm thinking about her."

"I will. Goodbye, Raina."

After hanging up with Phillip, I called Sal.

"I'm so glad to hear from you," he said. "I was really worried last night."

"I'm fine."

"You know, I stopped by your apartment. Someone was waiting for you there."

My eyes opened wide in surprise. "What are you talking about?"

"Tank. The leader of the Gold Vipers. He was hiding out in your apartment."

I sighed. "He never mentioned that."

"You spoke to him?"

"Yes."

"Did you tell him where Cole was?"

"No. Sal, I have something to tell you. You're not going to like it."

"What's wrong, honey?"

I took a deep breath and went over everything, including how I'd shot Slammer at the ATM. "So, I'm turning myself in," I said at the end. "To the police."

He groaned. "What? Why?"

"What do you mean, *why*? I murdered someone Sal. You of all people must realize how wrong that is."

"I do, but Raina... Slammer isn't worth going to jail for. I've been talking to people and they say he was definitely involved with some shady stuff."

"It doesn't matter. I killed him. He didn't deserve to die. Hell, don't what I was thinking. I killed a man in cold blood," I said miserably.

"It appears that way. But, you obviously reacted out of anger and grief. Hell, even Tank realizes that you weren't in control of your own actions."

"I *was* in control," I argued. "I wanted someone to die and he did. Now, I'm going to do the right thing."

"Sweetheart, do you have any idea how many years they'll lock you up for? You have to reconsider."

"I have to do this," I said softly.

He sighed. "And you're going to do it today?"

"Yes."

"At least let me see you before you turn yourself in. Please."

"I'll stop by the bar but don't try and talk me out of it, Sal. It won't work. I need to do this."

"I understand," he replied softly.

"I'm sorry I let you down. I know you wanted me to take over the bar."

"You didn't let me down. I let myself down."

I frowned. "Why do you say that?"

"Because, I was so wound up in my own demons that I had no idea how much more horrible yours actually were. Now, it's too late. I've failed."

"You did not fail," I said firmly. "My heart broke when Billy died and there is nothing you could have done that would have stopped me from going after the person I thought was responsible for his death. Don't you dare go blaming yourself. I'm a grown woman and liable for my own actions, Uncle Sal."

"Still –"

"Still, *nothing*. I did this to myself. I'm owning up to this, okay?"

"Yes," he replied, his voice sounding suddenly thick.

I rubbed my forehead. "You're not drinking, are you?"

"No," he said. "I'm just… emotional. Hold on." I heard him blowing his nose. When he was done, he sighed again. "Sorry about that."

"Don't be. I'm going to clean up around here and then meet you at the bar. Okay?"

"Sure."

"I love you, Sal."

"I love you, too, honey," he answered, sounding as if he was going to really start crying.

Feeling guilty, I hung up and began cleaning up some of the mess in my apartment, knowing that I might not see it again for quite a long time. As I was shoving an empty pizza box into a garbage bag, my phone rang.

"What now?" I mumbled, racing over to my purse. I pulled out my cell phone and saw that it was Joanna calling again. Sighing, I answered it.

"Raina. I need you to come and pick me up. Right now," she said quickly.

"What's going on?" I asked. "I spoke to Phillip earlier and he said some things..."

She laughed coldly. "Yeah, I'm sure he did. He's probably worried about what I told you."

"He said that you had a nervous breakdown."

"Don't listen to him. He'll say anything to keep his little secret. I'm surprised that I'm still breathing, to be honest."

"What are you talking about?" I asked, feeling frightened for her. "You're not saying that Phillip would physically harm you?

"To stay out of jail, I wouldn't put it past him."

"I don't even know what to say," I replied. "This just sounds too unbelievable. I'm sorry."

"I know it sounds crazy but we've known each other for over three years. You know I'm not crazy."

I'd *thought* she wasn't. Now, I wasn't so sure.

As if reading my mind, she let out a ragged sigh. "You have to believe me, Raina. Billy is alive. After what I saw, last night, I know he is."

"I'm sorry. This is just…" my voice trailed off.

"Hon, I saw him with my own eyes. I did. Now, if you ever want to see your son again, we've got to get back to the cabin, before Phillip moves the boy somewhere else"

TWENTY ONE

TANK

I WAS BREWING MYSELF a pot of coffee when Raptor and Tail showed up just after nine a.m.

"They certainly did a number on your windows," said Tail, walking through the doorway. "Good thing you weren't in your usual spot on the couch jerking off to pornos or you'd be dead, brother."

"Good thing your mother wasn't in *her* usual spot, down there on the carpet, blowing me. We'd both be goners," I answered, grinning back.

Tail flipped me off.

"This is some serious shit," said Raptor, examining some of the bullet holes in the side of the wall. "And you said the neighbors called the cops?"

"Yeah," I replied.

"Are they investigating?" asked Raptor.

"I don't know. They recovered most of the bullets and said they'd be looking into this, but I told them I wasn't interested in pressing charges."

"I'm sure they weren't expecting that," said Tail, plopping down into an oversized recliner that used to be Slammer's.

"Actually, they were," I replied, rubbing the back of my neck. It was still sore from sleeping on the sofa. "They know we'll handle this our way. Like we usually do."

"What about the girl? Raina?" asked Raptor, picking up a piece of glass I'd missed from the carpeting.

I shrugged. "Like I said last night, she's suffered enough, with her kid being killed."

"But, she murdered your old man," said Tail, looking up at me.

135

"Are you really just going to let that slide?"

"What do you propose I do? Rough her up? Put a bullet through her head? Toss her into a pit of snakes?" I replied testily.

"You could have her ass thrown in jail," he said. "She shouldn't get away with killing Slammer that easily."

I stared at him for several seconds and then smiled. "I like you. Your dedication to this club is already shining through."

"Thanks. I just think he was a great guy. He deserves some kind of retribution."

"And that he will get," I said. "When I find and kill the fucker who set him up. I know it was probably the leader of the Davenport Chapter, but I'm not going on assumptions. I need to find out for sure. I'm sure Cole knows. We just need to find him."

"What if he doesn't talk?" asked Tail.

"Oh, he will," I replied.

Raptor, who was thumbing through a girly magazine, looked over at me. "Raina tell you where he is?"

"No, but we know where she is. In fact, I want you two to find a cage and follow her around. Something tells me he's going to meet up with her, today."

"What if he doesn't?" asked Tail.

"Then we shadow her until he does," I replied.

Raptor stood up. "We'd better get moving then. You have an address for us?"

I grabbed a piece of paper and wrote it down. "She drives a newer Impala. It's silver," I said. Raina hadn't noticed when I'd followed her back to her vehicle which she'd parked down the street.

She'd sat there for a while, talking to someone on the phone before finally leaving.

Raptor took the slip of paper from me. "Okay. We'll stay in touch."

"Appreciate it," I said.

He gave me a quick hug. "You doing okay?" Raptor asked quietly.

I nodded. "It's strange but, now that I know who killed him and why, I feel like the real victim in all of this was Raina."

"That is strange," he said.

"I mean, don't get me wrong... I miss my old man. I miss him like hell. But, I had a lot of years with him. Good ones. Raina only had a few with her kid, Billy. She's barely hanging in there, now. I could see it in her eyes."

Raptor stared off into space. "Yeah, I can't imagine what I'd do if something like that had happened to my son. Probably go after the entire charter, myself, guns blazing."

"We need to find out who set up Slammer. We also need to find her son's killers," I said. "Something tells me that it's the only way she's going to move forward."

"Why do you care about this chick so much?" asked Tail. "Especially after what she did?"

I shrugged. "I don't know. I can't explain it. I just feel impelled to help her out."

"That's why he's our new Prez," said Raptor, squeezing my shoulder. "He's got a heart almost as big as his balls."

"I find that hard to believe," chuckled Tail.

I smirked. "Ask your mother. She'll tell you."

He flipped me off again.

TWENTY TWO

RAINA

J OANNA, BILLY IS dead," I said, blinking back tears. "I *saw* his body. His ashes are right in front of me." I picked up the urn and ran my thumb over it. "I don't know what you think you saw, but it wasn't my Billy."

"Do you remember last Christmas, when Phillip was talking about his friend Jacob Sleffer?"

"No. I'm sorry, I guess I don't."

"I didn't think so, but I thought I'd ask. Jacob Sleffer is a chemist. He works for this big-time pharmaceutical company, Fairfield Enterprises. Anyway, Phillip mentioned that Sleffer was testing some new drug that could actually make one appear as if they were dead."

I clutched the phone tightly. "Really?"

"Yes. Something containing tetrodotoxin, I believe."

"Sorry, I don't know what that is."

"It's something that's found in puffer fish. Apparently it's deadly, but Sleffer has been experimenting with it and last fall, he created a powder that not only slows a person's heartrate, but paralyzes them so that they don't react to any stimuli."

"You can't really think that they used this powder on Billy?" I asked, the blood rushing to my ears. It seemed like a crazy notion, but the mother inside of me wanted to believe anything that might bring my son back to me.

"I know they did. I saw him with my own eyes. It was your boy. I know it."

"Why would Phillip use it on Billy?" I asked, thinking back to the night Billy was rushed to the Emergency Room. By the time I'd made it there, Phillip and Joanna had already been there, in the waiting room. "And *how*?"

"Why?" She sighed. "I hate to say this, but ever since Mark died, Phillip has wanted custody of Billy."

"He's *my* son. Why would he want to try and get custody of his nephew?" I asked.

She sighed. "You know that we can't have children, don't you?"

"Actually, Phillip told me that. Today."

"I was fine with adopting, but he didn't want that. Instead, he wanted Billy. He has always believed that you're an unfit mother, and when the shooting incident occurred, I think it must have sent him into action."

"You really believe that Billy is alive?" I asked, sitting down.

"I do. In fact, I saw Sleffer that night at the hospital. I didn't think anything of it until I saw Billy at the cabin. When was the last time that you saw your son?"

"Early the next morning. They had to do an autopsy, because of the shooting. It was the last time I saw him," I said, remembering his pale little body, lying there in the hospital bed, before they wheeled him out. I'd been given only a few minutes alone with him afterward.

"Are you there?" she asked.

I cleared my throat. "I remember Billy's skin had still been a little warm. I hadn't thought too much about it since I was in shock. He had no pulse, though."

"The powder given to him would have made him appear that way. He had a pulse, believe me."

"But, Phillip wasn't the surgeon who'd been working on Billy. You can't tell me that they're all in on this?"

"All I know is that Phillip left the waiting room for a while before you got there. To check on Billy, he said. Maybe he delivered the powder without anyone knowing."

"This sounds like something out of a movie," I said, wondering who was crazier. Her, for telling me this story. Or me, for considering it.

"Life is sometimes stranger than fiction. He's alive. Now, just like I said before. We have to get up to the cabin before Phillip moves him."

I stood up quickly. "Where are you?"

"I'm at Shultz's drug store. The place on Cannon Drive."

"I thought Phillip had someone watching over you."

She snickered. "Yeah. He did. A woman, from the hospital. Supposedly she's some nurse. Anyway, the old bat gave me a sedative to swallow, but I didn't really take it."

"Where is she now?" I asked, worried that the nurse would call Phillip.

"On her laptop. She didn't even notice me leave."

"Okay," I replied. "I'm on my way."

"I'll be watching for you.

I hung up the phone, grabbed my purse, and rushed out of my apartment. It seemed so hard to believe that my son could be alive. But, if there was even a slight chance, there was no way that I'd let it slip through my fingers.

TWENTY THREE

TANK

I WAS JUST GETTING on my bike, when Raptor called me.

"She's on the move," he said.

I slipped my sunglasses on. "Okay. Follow her and let me know where she goes."

"Will do," he said, before hanging up.

I clipped my phone back onto my belt, started the engine, and drove to the clubhouse. When I arrived, Hoss and a few of the other guys started in on me right away, asking about the drive-by.

"They did some minor damage, but fortunately, nobody was hurt," I said and then smiled coldly. "Someone will be, however, when I find out who it was."

"You have any idea?" asked Hoss, lighting a cigarette.

"I'm sure it was the Devil's Rangers, but I need proof before I come down on them. Jesus, didn't I tell you to smoke outside from now on?" I said, waving it away.

"This isn't the gym, Popeye," he replied, smirking. "Just because you're trying to quit smoking, doesn't mean we all have to cross the parking lot for a few puffs."

Hoss was in his fifties and looked closer to seventy. He was a chain-smoker and there was hardly a minute that went by without the sound of him almost coughing up a lung. Unfortunately, he refused to see anyone about it. I'd asked him to quit smoking in the clubhouse, mainly because I was worried about him and thought he'd slow down a little. Unfortunately, he was as stubborn as his cough. "That hacking of yours is getting worse. You should see a doctor."

"Now you sound like my old lady. Let me tell you something,

Tank, I'll see a fucking doctor, but only when he's standing over me and pronouncing my time of death," he said in his gravelly voice. "Until then, I'm not seeing any of those quacks."

I sighed. "Fine. Can you at least try one of those vapor cigarettes? Aren't they supposed to be better for your health?"

"I don't know but I'm not smoking those yuppie things," he said, blowing out another stream of smoke. "Hell, Slammer would turn over laughing in his grave if I started smoking those things. Maybe even fucking poltergeist me or some shit. I'm sticking with what I know and enjoy."

Hoss had been one of Slammer's closest friends. I knew enough to let it be. Out of respect. If he wanted to kill himself, that was up to him. "Fine. I get the point."

"For all you know, those things could be injecting you with something that makes you crave what they're selling even more so. Or hell, maybe that's how the government is going to control everyone in the future." His eyes grew really wide. "Right over the counter, too. You purchase a refill of that liquid stuff and who knows what you're really inhaling."

Some of the guys chuckled.

"Hey, laugh all you want, but someday, you'll know. It's the beginning of the end. They're going to control us one way or another," he said. "It's nothing but a damn conspiracy."

"Conspiracy or not, let's get back to what we can control," I said, knowing that if someone didn't stop him, he'd be on a roll. "Or at least try to. I was going to hold church later, but I want to start getting to the bottom of the drive-by as soon as possible."

"The one at your place?" asked Horse.

"That… and the one we were blamed for a couple of weeks ago. The snipers who shot up the Devil's Rangers party."

"Why in the fuck are we looking into that?" asked Buck. "I mean, they probably did us a favor, right?"

"The only person killed during that raid was a child," I said, frowning. "From what I hear, everyone else recovered."

"Oh hell, I had no idea," replied Buck, looking ashamed. "Sorry."

"It's all good, brother," I said, squeezing his shoulder. "But, this shit needs to be stopped and the hell if we're going to be blamed for murdering a kid. That's why we need to find out who's behind it."

"Agreed," he replied.

"So, I want you all to start asking around town. See if anyone knows anything," I said, looking around.

They all agreed.

My cell phone began to buzz. I looked at a text from Raptor, telling me that Raina had picked up some chick and now they were heading out of town.

Good. Maybe they'll lead you to Cole, I texted back.

Will let you know.

Sounds good. Keep me in the loop.

I was putting my phone away when Frannie called.

"I heard about what happened," she said, sounding worried. "Are you okay?"

"I'm fine. A couple of broken windows. No big deal."

"No big deal? You could have been killed."

"If I'm going to die, it's not going to be from some drive-by," I said.

145

She let out a ragged sigh. "Why don't you come and stay with me and Jessica? She's worried about you, too."

I smiled. "Look, I appreciate your concern, but I'm not letting something like that drive me from my home. Plus, how would it look for the president of our club to be running home to mommy?"

"You might be worried about your reputation, but I'm more worried about your life," she scolded.

I scratched my chin. I'd forgotten to shave. "Relax. I'm not going to be alone tonight. There will be a couple of prospects posted outside my door, keeping watch," I said in a low voice. The last thing I needed was for anyone to hear me talking to my stepmother about needing protection. I certainly didn't think I needed any, but I knew she wouldn't leave it rest until I placated her.

"Good. I want you to stop by tonight for dinner. Jessica is trying out some meatloaf recipe."

"She's cooking?" I asked, surprised. "I thought she didn't like to."

"Normally, no. All of a sudden she's 'Betty Homemaker'. Making me breakfast, lunch, dinner. She's been going onto Pinterest and searching for recipes, too. I think she's worried about me," said Frannie, her voice trailing off.

I remembered the way Jessica been making out with the Judge the other night. Something told me her sudden interest in cooking had more to do with him. "What's Pinterest?"

"Oh, it's a website for sharing stuff."

"Huh," I said, not really interested. I normally couldn't sit in front of a computer for more than fifteen minutes without getting frustrated or antsy. Hell, I couldn't sit in front of television for very long, either, which is why I had it on in my workout room in the basement.

She laughed. "I've lost you already, haven't I?"

"You know me. I'm not into surfing the web or any of that crap."

"I know. But you are into eating, so be here by seven if you want to try Jessica's meatloaf. She'll be hurt if you don't show up."

"I'll be there," I promised.

"Good. We'll see you then."

"Okay."

After we hung up, I went into the office and sat down in Slammer's old leather chair, which still had cigarette burns on the armrest. I leaned back, closed my eyes, and thought about the picture I'd seen in Raina's apartment of her kid. He'd obviously been the apple of her eye and the fact that she'd gone after the person she thought had been responsible for killing him, made perfect sense. I couldn't even really blame her for killing my old man. She'd been used like a pawn. I wasn't exactly sure who the real opponent was yet, but I was bound and determined to find and bury the motherfucker.

TWENTY FOUR

RAINA

WHEN I PICKED up Joanna, she was nervous as all hell. "I'm sorry it took so long to get here," I said, watching her put the seatbelt on.

"It's fine. Let's get out of here," she replied, looking around nervously.

"Don't you think that nurse is going to find you missing and call Phillip?"

"I put some pillows under the blanket. Hopefully, she won't figure it out for several hours."

"How far away is your cabin?" I asked, pulling out of the parking lot.

"Only two hours. We'll need to take the I-80 West. It's in Waterloo."

"Okay," I replied.

"That's right, you've never been there."

"No," I replied, not surprised now that I knew how much of an asshole Phillip really was.

As if reading my mind, she smiled. "Don't take it personally. He never allowed anyone there, and Lord knows how many times I asked to invite you and Billy. He's not much of a people person."

"He's a snob," I said.

She laughed grimly. "Yes. He certainly is. I used to think it was kind of cute, if you can believe it."

"Cute?" I repeated, frowning. "What's cute about thinking you're better than everyone else?"

Joanna sat back in the chair and stared into the distance. "You're right. It's not. I guess I was so enamored by him when we first met that I excused everything. Now, I'd love to back over him with his new Bentley."

149

"I thought you two had a great relationship," I said, turning onto the highway.

She tapped her fingers on the door. "So did I. The last few months, however, he's been a bear to live with. I'm not sure if it was Mark's death or the fact that we weren't able to conceive our own child, that's made him so intolerable. He's been spending so much time alone at the cabin, that I thought maybe he was having an affair. Now I know what he's been up to, I'd almost prefer the cheating. No offense. I want Billy to be alive, but knowing that Phillip did something like this… it's horrifying, to say the least."

"You've got that right. He's going to prison, if what you say is true." Although, as far as I was concerned, Phillip deserved much worse.

"I know. Hell, I know more than anyone," she mumbled.

"When you saw Billy, at the cabin, was there anyone else besides Phillip staying there?"

"I imagine there was, although I didn't see anyone at the time. Someone has to be staying with Billy while Phillip is back in town."

"Speaking of which, what did he say when you confronted him about it?"

"He told me that the boy in the cabin was the housekeeper's son."

"You have a housekeeper for your cabin?" I asked incredulously.

"Believe me, it was news to my ears, too. He claims that he hired one because the place was getting dusty and needed a good cleaning."

"Are you sure it *wasn't* the housekeeper's kid?" I asked, wondering if we were on a wild goose chase.

"I'm positive. I know what I saw and it was your son," she replied firmly.

"But, you saw him from outside, right?"

She looked over at me and smiled. "You'd have made a great lawyer."

"I doubt it. My judgement of people is pretty shitty these days."

"I'm certain that it was Billy. I got a good look inside and there's no doubt in my mind of who it was playing Legos."

"Okay," I said, wanting to believe it, but frightened that I'd be getting my hopes up for nothing. "I just hope that Phillip didn't move him to another location."

"I hope not, too. After he told me about the housekeeper's kid, I pretended to believe him. I don't know if I fooled him or not, though."

"I guess we'll find out."

"I guess so."

BOTH OF US were quiet for much of the ride. After a while, she fell asleep and it wasn't until we entered Waterloo that I tapped her on the shoulder.

"Oh," she said, blinking. "We're here already."

"Yeah," I replied, my stomach a ball of knots now that our destination was in reach. I could barely concentrate on the driving. All I could think about was finding Billy alive and ripping Phillip's head off if I did.

Joanna sat up straight. "Okay, you're going to want to stay on this road for about two more miles. When you get to Wild Prairie Road, you'll take a right."

"Okay," I replied, gripping the steering wheel tightly.

She frowned. "Do you want me to drive?"

"Actually, that might be a good idea," I said, pulling over to the side of the road. "You know the area anyway."

We got out and switched sides.

"What if Phillip is there?" I asked, grabbing my purse from the backseat. I still had the gun hidden inside "When I spoke to him earlier, he said he was at the hospital, but he could have been lying."

"All I know is that he had two operations scheduled today. That's what he said, anyway," she replied.

I pulled the handgun out of my purse.

"Jesus, what are you doing with that thing?" she exclaimed.

"You said so yourself – Phillip was dangerous," I replied, checking the chamber.

"Do you have a permit for that?"

I looked at her and raised my eyebrows. "Really?"

"Sorry. It's the lawyer in me."

"This gun isn't registered to me. I don't have a permit. If we end up shooting the bastard, in self-defense of course, I'll tell the police that we found the gun in the cabin. Just back my story."

She nodded. "God, this is crazy."

Something told me that it was going to get much crazier...

TWENTY FIVE

TANK

AFTER NOT HEARING from Raptor for two hours, I decided to call him. For some reason, I couldn't get Raina out of my mind and was curious as to what she was up to and if she'd met up with Cole. "What's going on?"

"We're in Waterloo, Iowa," he said.

"Really?"

"Yeah."

"She hasn't spotted you?"

"I don't think so."

"Okay. Call me back when you know something more."

"Okay."

I hung up the phone and decided to take a drive over to Griffin's to check on things. When I arrived, Cheeks was there, managing the bar.

"Hey, hot stuff," she said, happy to see me. "Want a beer?"

"No, I'm not staying," I replied, looking toward the stage. It was Happy Hour and the place was packed. "New stripper?"

"Yeah. Don't you recognize her?"

"No," I replied.

"Try looking at her face," she said with a smirk.

I tore my eyes away from her tits, which were on the smaller size but damn perky. "She looks familiar," I said, looking at her profile. The girl had long, dark brown hair that was pulled back into a ponytail and pink, glossy lips. She reminded me a little of Raina, only not quite as sexy.

"It's my niece. Layla."

My eyes widened. "What? Your niece? Isn't she underage?"

"She was three years ago," said Cheeks, "which was the last time you saw her. She just turned twenty-one last week."

"She's filled out nicely," I replied, remembering the way I'd been checking her out the last time I'd seen her. Now that she was legal and working in my bar, I thought I'd have been more stoked about getting down her pants. But surprisingly, she wasn't doing anything other than making me think of Raina.

"She has a major crush you," said Cheeks, nodding toward Layla. "Be warned."

"You're warning me?" I asked, chuckling. "Shouldn't you be warning her about me?"

"If I had, she'd be in your bed before her next dance."

"I'm sure she's a real nice girl, but you know me, Cheeks," I said, grabbing her ass. "I like my women with more meat on their bones."

She smiled in pleasure and grabbed my crotch. "And you already know how I feel about your meat, big guy."

I leaned over and whispered in her ear. "Actually, I don't think I *do* remember. You have some extra time to remind me?"

As if on cue, a large group of guys entered the bar. She groaned. "How about a raincheck?"

"No problem," I said, adjusting myself. "If the customers are happy, they spend more money, which," I smiled, "makes the owner happy. Go make some money, darlin'."

She winked and walked over to serve the newcomers.

I glanced at Layla, who was finishing up her school-girl routine, and went into the back to use the bathroom. When I was finished, I headed toward the business office.

"Hi, Tank," said a voice behind me.

I turned around and found Layla standing there, wearing a pink bra and matching G-string. She was holding a handful of money in one hand and a red plaid skirt in the other.

"Hi, Layla," I answered, her perfume or body-spray scent filling the hallway. It reminded me of cotton candy.

She smiled. "I wasn't sure if you remembered me."

"Of course I do, darlin'," I replied, smiling. "How could I forget?"

Layla walked toward me. "I'm so sorry to hear about your dad."

"Thanks."

With a sympathetic look, she threw her arms around my waist and hugged me. "I hope you catch that person who did it," she said, resting her cheek against my chest.

I awkwardly patted Layla on the back. "I'm working on it."

"He was such a sweet guy."

"I wasn't aware that you knew him all that well."

"I didn't. But, my aunt said he was one of the nicest guys she'd ever met."

"Nice?" I repeated, smiling. "He'd roll over in his grave if he heard the word being used to describe him."

Layla, who was still holding onto me, pressed her body into mine. "So, I saw you watching me on stage," she murmured. "It turned me on."

"Watching you is part of my job, sweetheart," I said, grabbing her right hand, which was moving dangerously close to my zipper. "I have to make sure you're doing yours."

"Was I?"

"Definitely."

"Did it turn you on?"

I didn't reply.

She looked up at me, a wicked expression on her face. "I think it did. One thing is for certain, you turned me on," she said, sliding her other hand over my bulge. "So does what's trying to get out. Are you circumcised?"

Torn between taking her back to the office and fucking the shit out of her or running like hell, I clenched my jaw and brushed her hand away. "Stop, Layla…"

"But why? Do you have any idea how long I've been waiting to get together with you?" she pouted, now rubbing her chest against the front of my cut.

I groaned. As horny as she was making me, I knew it would be wrong to bang the girl. Especially since her aunt and I were sometimes fuck-buddies. "Listen, sweetness, I'm flattered. I am. But, now that I own this place, I need to keep my relationships platonic with the girls working here," I lied.

Her face fell. "Seriously?"

I wasn't about to tell her about Cheeks. "Yes. Sorry, darlin'."

Sighing, Layla stepped back and then bent down to pick up some of the dollars she'd dropped. "Fine, but you don't know what you're missing."

Watching her tight little ass bending down to pick up the bills made what I was missing abundantly clear. Not trusting myself to say 'no' again, I turned and began heading toward the office. "I'm sure you're right, but business is business. By the way, keep up the good work," I called back to her.

"Thanks," she answered, still glowering.

My cell phone buzzed as soon as I walked into the office. When I saw that it was Tail, I answered quickly. "What's up?"

"Some shit is going down."

"Talk to me," I said, closing my door.

"We followed Raina and her friend to this cabin in Waterloo and they disappeared inside. Shortly after, we heard gunfire.

I swore. "Where's Raptor?"

"He's checking it out. Told me to call you."

"Okay. Go help Raptor. I'm heading your way."

He gave me quick directions. After we hung up, I grabbed my keys and rushed out of the bar.

TWENTY SIX

RAINA

A S WE NEARED Joanna and Phillip's log cabin, she slowed the car down.

"Look, there's a car parked outside. It was there last night, next to Phillip's," she said, pointing up the dirt road.

It was a newer red BMW. "And you're not sure whose it is?"

"No. I thought it was someone he was having an affair with, but I left so fast, I didn't get a chance to see the owner."

"Maybe this person is the one caring for Billy?"

"That's what I'm wondering. I'm parking back here. They'll see us if we get too close," she said, pulling behind some trees.

Catching another glimpse of the home, I couldn't help but feel like I was very much out of my element. The cabin, which had to be over ten-thousand square feet, looked like something out of an architectural magazine.

"This place is breathtaking," I said, staring at the large, rustic retreat.

"Thanks. It took two years to build," she said, shutting off the car.

"I bet," I replied, feeling a stab of envy. I could never provide such a luxurious home for Billy and it made me feel so inadequate.

"I know. It looks a little overwhelming," admitted Joanna. "And, honestly, I think it's too much for just the two of us. I wanted something cozy and quaint, but Phillip insisted on going big." She smirked. "Probably because he lacks in size, if you get my drift."

I smiled. "That explains a lot."

"Well, are you ready?" she asked, holding out the keys to me.

I grabbed them.

"Let's go and find your son."

Dropping the keys into my purse, I pulled out the gun. "Let's go."

She frowned. "Do you know how to use that thing?"

"Yes."

She sighed. "If this goes bad, I wasn't here. I foresee a divorce in my near future, and I can't afford to lose my job."

"I understand," I said, getting out of the vehicle.

Joanna got out, too, and we began making our way to the back of the cabin. When we reached the door, she pulled a set of keys out of her purse. "This is crazy, but I shouldn't be so nervous about going into my own home. I'm really beginning to hate Phillip for making me feel this way."

"Welcome to the club."

She slid the key into the door and let out a ragged breath. "Okay. Here goes nothing."

I watched as Joanna unlocked the door and then followed her inside to an impressive entertainment area. Not only was there an eighty-inch projector television, but they had twelve leather loungers facing it. There was also a popcorn machine behind the seating area, and a soda dispenser.

"Obviously, this is our media room," she said, closing the door behind us. "We've never used it, but Phillip insisted that we needed something like this."

"It's nice," I replied. "And I love that smell." The giant room smelled like cedar and leather.

"I used to, but quite honestly, it's making me sick to my stomach," she said, looking around. "All of it. You know, the more that I learn about my husband, the more nauseous I become."

I didn't know how to respond, since I couldn't stand him myself.

"Come on. Let's go search the rest of the house."

I followed her out and we quietly checked the remaining rooms in the basement. Not finding anyone, we headed toward the staircase.

She turned around and looked at me. "This will lead into the kitchen. So be prepared," she whispered.

"I'm surprised you don't have a security system," I whispered back as we started up the stairs.

"He's been meaning to get one installed. You hear that?" she whispered, stopping abruptly.

There were muffled voices coming from the other side of the door.

"I think it's the TV," I whispered.

"There's one in the kitchen."

I recognized the music and voices from a television show Billy adored, *Dora, the Explorer*. Then we both heard the sound of a young child laughing.

"I told you. It's him. He's here," she whispered, beaming a smile at me

I quickly went around her, needing to see if my son was actually in the house.

"Wait," she whispered loudly.

Ignoring Joanna, I cracked the door open slightly and peeked through. The first thing I noticed was a woman sitting down at the kitchen island, engrossed in a book. She appeared to be in her fifties, had white hair, and was dressed to the nines. Something about her was familiar, but I wasn't sure what. Feeling more courageous, I opened the door a little wider and that's when I almost fell backwards to my death. My two-year-old son, the love of my life, was seated in a high chair, watching television and eating crackers. His left arm was in some kind of a sling, but other than that, he was alive and breathing.

My eyes filled with tears. "Oh, my God... Billy!" I gasped, flinging the door open. I rushed over to where he was seated and set the gun down to free him from the high-chair.

"Mommy," he cried happily, raising his right hand to me as I pulled the plastic top off.

"You get away from him," snapped the older woman, coming to life.

"Raina, watch out," said Joanna in a strangled voice.

I looked over my shoulder and found myself staring into the barrel of a gun.

"Mommy," whined Billy, trying to get the seatbelt off by himself. "Out."

"Put the gun down," I said, furious at myself for putting mine down.

"Back away from him," she said, ignoring me. "*Now.*"

"No. This is my son and there is nothing you can do to make me leave him," I said, my voice shaky.

"Betty, what in the hell are you doing?" said Joanna, taking a step closer to her.

It was then that I recognized the woman. She was Phillip and Mark's estranged aunt. Mark had mentioned a few times that the woman was crazy. I'd never suspected just how much.

"You stay out of this," ordered Betty, waving the gun back and forth between the two of us now. "Jake!" she cried loudly.

Not understanding why I wasn't getting him out of the high-chair, Billy began to cry.

"It's okay," I said, turning away from Betty again. As threatening as she was, I could tell by the look in her eyes that she wouldn't actually shoot me. At least, I hoped I was reading that correctly.

"You're insane," said Joanna. "Do you know how much trouble you're in?"

"Shut up," she replied. "And you... get away from him."

Only half-listening, I unbuckled Billy and pulled him up and into my arms, trying to be careful with his arm. He rested his head on my shoulder and I kissed his cheek, my tears sliding off of my nose, onto his nose. He had fever, which worried me. Especially since I didn't know what was under his bandage.

"Mommy, that tickles," he said, giggling, as more of my tears dripped onto his skin.

"Sorry, sweetheart. Does your arm hurt a lot?"

His smile fell and he nodded.

I kissed his forehead, relishing in the baby shampoo scent I'd missed so much. At least they'd kept him clean and fed. "We'll bring you to a doctor and see if they can help you feel better."

"Okay," Billy replied and then turned to Joanna. "Hi."

"Hi. Goodness, you poor little guy," said Joanna, her eyes soft. "Your mommy is here now. She'll take good care of you."

"Yes. Thanks to you," I said, unable to thank her enough.

"I'm just relieved that he was still here."

"Me, too." Although, the thought of what he must have gone through during the last couple of weeks made me both angry and frustrated. I looked over at Joanna. "Let's get him out of here."

"Stop where you are," said a man's voice firmly.

Stiffening up, I turned around and saw a balding, middle-aged man, with glasses, pointing a revolver at me.

"Well if it isn't the medical genius himself," said Joanna dryly. "This is the guy I was telling you about, Raina. Jacob Slether."

I gritted my teeth. "You're the man whose been experimenting with my child?"

"Put the boy down or I'll shoot you in the head. Right in front of your son."

The thought of Billy witnessing that made me hesitate. "You're really going to shoot someone carrying a child?"

"If you don't put the boy down, yes. Most definitely. I'm actually a very good shot. Betty," he said, much louder, "you'd better call Phillip."

She reached for the cell phone, sitting on the dark granite counter, and began searching for the number.

"Put the gun down before someone gets hurt," said Joanna, talking a couple of steps toward him. "I'm sure Phillip would be extremely angry with you if you hurt Billy, even if it was by accident."

"Get back," he said, cocking the gun. "Or you'll be the one who gets hurt."

She raised her hands in the air and gave him a dirty look. "Fine. Just be careful with that thing."

He waved the gun back toward me. "We have a plane to catch soon and I've got no time for games. Now, you put the child down or I'll shoot Joanna."

"What?" I gasped.

"Mommy... I want to go home," moaned Billy, putting his fingers into his mouth. He laid his head down on my shoulder once again.

"I know, honey. I know." Determined not to leave without my son, I looked back at Slether. "Listen to me, if you just let us leave, we won't say a word. I swear to God."

He laughed coldly. "Right."

"I'm serious. I don't want anything to do with the law. I just want to take my son home. Please, let us go."

"Sorry, but that's not going to happen. Now listen, I'll give you ten seconds to put the kid down or I'll just start shooting. One... two..."

Before he could make it to 'three', Joanna ran out of the room, screaming her head off as a distraction. It was almost comical.

"Dammit," growled Slether. "Betty, stay here with them."

She picked up the gun from the counter and pointed it at me again. Slether ran off.

Still not believing that she'd fire the gun at us, I decided to act. I held onto Billy as tight as I could and ran toward the basement.

She gasped. "Stop! Jake! She's getting away!"

I made it to the stairs and raced down, frantic to get my son out of the cabin. As I took the last step, I heard someone following me. Thinking it was Betty, I glanced over my shoulder and to my dismay, found that it was Slether coming after me.

"No," I mumbled, running toward the media room. Before I could make it, Slether fired the gun, shooting me in the thigh. Crying out in pain, I stumbled to the ground while trying not to land on my son. The next thing I knew, he was pulling Billy out of my arms.

"Mommy!" cried Billy.

"Let him go, you bastard!" I screamed, watching in horror as Slether ran away with my son.

Using all of my strength, I got back to my feet and limped over to the stairs, frantic to get Billy back.

"I don't think so," said Betty, standing at the top, her gun pointed down toward me. "You aren't getting him back and we don't need any witnesses."

I raised my hand. "Please. He's my son," I begged. "You can't do this."

"It's already been done," she said smirking.

I stared past her and saw Joanna coming up behind Betty. She shoved the older woman forward, sending her tumbling down the steps. Horrified, I got out of the way, as she landed near my feet, her neck broken.

"Hurry!" called Joanna, turning away from the stairs. "Before he gets away!"

Lightheaded and in a world of hurt, I climbed up, focusing on nothing else but getting my son back. As I reached the top of the staircase, I heard the sound of an automatic garage door. Panicking, I stumbled through the cabin, toward the front door. When I made it outside and onto the porch, I saw a red SUV kicking up dust as it headed away from the house.

Slether was getting away.

"No!" I screamed, dropping to my knees.

"Bullshit. I'm not letting him get away with this!" hollered Joanna. She began running toward my car, as if there was still a chance in hell that they could be stopped.

But then a miracle happened – an old pickup truck pulled out of the woods and slammed into the front of Slether's vehicle, halting it.

I gasped in surprise.

A blonde guy jumped out of the truck, pointing a shotgun toward the SUV.

"Don't fire!" I screamed, horrified. I got to my feet and limped toward them. "My son is in there!"

"Get your hands in the air and get out of the truck or I'll blow your fucking head off!" ordered the man, his gun trained on the driver's side window.

Instead of obeying, Slether tried starting the SUV, but the engine wouldn't turn over.

Pissed off, the stranger shot his gun, hitting the side-mirror. "Don't fuck with me, asshole. Get out, now!"

I breathed a sigh of relief when I saw the door open and Slether get out, his arms in the air.

Another guy ran past me, coming from God knows where. "Stay back, Raina," he called over his shoulder.

Recognizing the patch on the back of his cut, I didn't know whether to be grateful or pissed off.

"Who are those guys?" asked Joanna, jogging back to me.

"They belong to a biker club. The Gold Vipers," I mumbled, wondering what they were doing there.

"Are they on our side?" she asked as we watched them get Slether out of the SUV.

"I guess we're going to find out soon enough," I said, limping toward them.

TWENTY SEVEN

TANK

I DROVE LIKE A bat out of hell on my bike, reaching Waterloo around six p.m. When I finally made it to the cabin, the cops were there. One of them was interviewing Tail on the porch, who nodded when he saw me. I nodded back.

"Hey," said Raptor, walking over to me. "Some crazy shit, huh?"

"Sounds like it. Where's Raina?" I asked, looking around.

"She's already gone. They took her to the hospital."

"Is she okay?" I asked. I knew she'd been shot and was worried about her.

"Sounds like she'll be fine. The bullet only grazed the outside of her thigh," he replied. "She'll be sore for a while, but nothing major to worry about."

"What about her boy? Billy?" I asked, still in shock that he was alive.

"Joanna took him to the hospital, to be with his mother. There's an APB out for the guy responsible for kidnapping him. Phillip Davis."

"The brother-in-law?"

"Yep."

"Is that Dr. Frankenstein?" I asked, nodding toward one of the squad cars. There was a man in the back, watching us.

"Yes. There was also an older woman involved. Apparently, Slether pushed her down the steps. He's denying it, but both women swear he did it."

I rubbed the back of my neck. "You think that's the truth?"

"Honestly, I don't know."

"Which hospital did they take her?"

"Saint Rose's."

171

I pulled my phone out to get directions. "I'm going to head over there. Are you going to need a ride back to Jensen?" I asked, glancing at pickup. "We could call a couple of the prospects to drive out here and pick you up."

"Adriana is already on her way."

"Okay."

Tail walked over a few seconds later.

"How'd that go?" I asked.

"Fine. Seemed like they had more questions about our club than anything else. Don't worry, Tank. I didn't make it worth their time."

"I wasn't worried," I replied. Tail, although sometimes rash in his decisions, was already proving to be loyal. Everyone seemed to like him, especially the club whores. They were already fighting over him.

"By the way, Adriana is picking us up," Raptor said to him.

"That's good. My truck is toast," replied Tail.

We all turned to look at it. The front corner was smashed and it was leaking something.

"Sorry, brother," I said. "We'll take care of you."

"It's okay," he replied. "I was thinking about buying a new one anyway. I need it for work."

Tail, and another member of the club, J.T., had recently started a small roofing company.

"Good. At least let me help you with the down payment on a new one. It's the least I can do."

He grinned. "Well, fuck, I can't say 'no' to that."

I put my hand on his shoulder. "That was quick thinking on your part. I'm proud of you."

Looking pleased, he waved his thumb toward the SUV. "I saw him taking off with the kid and knew something was cagy. I could have chased him down, but something told me that it would have ended badly."

"You made the right choice," I replied, as my phone began to ring. When I looked who was calling me, I swore.

"Are you on your way?" Frannie asked when I answered.

"Something came up," I told her. "I had to leave town."

She sighed. "Jessica worked hard on this meatloaf. She wanted to see your reaction."

"I'm sure it's fabulous. Tell her I'm sorry and will make it up to her."

"How about *you* tell her?"

Before I could argue, Jessica was on the phone with me.

"What's your excuse this time?" she teased.

Fortunately, my stepsister was too sweet to be a much of a bitch. "This time? What are you talking about?" I asked, lightheartedly.

"Seems like you're avoiding us, Tank," she said. "Especially my cooking."

"Believe me, I'd rather be seated at the table, eating your meatloaf, than what I'm doing now."

"Which is?"

"Let's just say that the club had to rescue a kid and reunite him with his mother."

She inhaled. "Really? You guys did that?"

"Well, Tail and Raptor did. Anyway, to make a long story short, I had to leave town, to join them. I won't be back until late tonight, I'm sure. Can I get a raincheck on dinner?"

"Of course. How about next Sunday? I've got a lot to do in the next few days, otherwise I'd make something else sooner."

"That would be great. Have you heard from the Judge lately?" I asked, still wondering what exactly was going on between the two of them.

"We've spoken on the phone a few times," she replied. "He has some things to take care of and then is supposed to return to Jensen."

"You two seemed pretty tight the other night."

"Yeah. I know," replied Jessica, a smile in her voice.

"What's going on?"

"To be honest, I'm not exactly sure," she replied. "But once I find out, you'll be the first to know."

"He'd better not be playin' my baby sister," I said, teasing her. "I'll have to hunt his ass down and take care of business."

"Don't worry. I'm pretty sure Jordan is not just out for sex. At least, I hope."

I heard Frannie gasp in the background.

"Mom, go away. Stop listening to our conversation," Jessica said, laughing. "What you don't know won't hurt you."

I heard some mumbling in the background, but wasn't sure what Frannie was saying.

"I gotta go," I said, looking back at Raptor who was watching me curiously. "I'll be at the dinner table on Sunday. You have my word."

"Okay. Hope you like fish, because I'm making salmon."

"Love salmon."

"Good. Talk to you later."

"Definitely."

"What was that about the Judge?" asked Raptor after I hung up.

"Oh, yeah… I'm surprised you didn't know. Your brother has been getting busy with Jessica."

He looked surprised. "Really? I'd heard that something had happened between them in Alaska, but wasn't sure."

"They've been talking on the phone, so it might be serious. From what you told me, he's not much of a conversationalist."

"No. He's not," Raptor said, looking amused.

"I don't know what he's been saying to her, but she sounds like she's on cloud-nine, the way she talks about him. Anyway, I'm outta here. You guys need anything, give me a call."

"Will do," said Raptor.

"See you back in Jensen," Tail said.

I walked back to my bike, got on, and headed toward the hospital.

TWENTY EIGHT

RAINA

"**M**OMMY, I WANNA go home," pouted Billy. He was sitting on Joanna's lap while we waited for the doctor to return. Fortunately, my wound wasn't as bad as I'd thought and had only required stitches. The bullet had barely grazed my leg.

"I know. We're almost done here," I said, squeezing his knee. "Then we'll go home."

"Did you bwing Bunny?"

Bunny, a brown floppy-eared rabbit, was his favorite stuffed animal and he'd dragged it around everywhere. I'd slept with it ever since the night Billy had been pronounced dead. "No. I'm sorry. But, he's waiting for you at home."

"I want him now," he demanded.

"Soon," I replied. "We're waiting for the doctor to write a prescription to help your ear." I'd already given him children's pain reliever medicine. Apparently, he really had been shot, but from what the doctor said, it looked like it was healing fairly well. As far as his temperature being high, the doctor had found that Billy had an ear infection and was going to prescribe medication for it.

"Daddy gave me some aweady," he said. "Last night."

"Honey, Uncle Phillip is not your daddy," I said, wanting to kill the son-of-a-bitch with my bare hands.

"He tole me to," Billy said.

"You have just one daddy. His name is Mark," I said, trying not to show how angry I really was.

"He's in Heaven," said Billy, repeating something he'd heard

177

quite a few times.

"Yes, baby," I replied, touching his cheek. "Your daddy is there. Someday you'll see him again."

He grinned. "Okay."

There was a knock at the door.

"Come in," I called, thinking it was the doctor returning.

A head peeked around the corner and I almost choked on my own saliva.

"Hi," said Justin. "Can I come in?"

"Uh, sure," I replied, raising my hand to my hair, which I knew was probably a mess.

Justin entered the room carrying a bundle of roses and a stuffed German Shepherd puppy. He grinned when he saw Billy sitting on Joanna's lap.

"Hey there, little guy. How are you doing?" he asked him.

"Okay. Whose puppy is dat?" Billy asked, pointing to the toy.

"I don't know. He followed me down the hallway, insisting that I find someone named Billy. I figured he was yours."

Billy shook his head. His eyes were wide. "No."

Justin walked over to the side of my bed and held the stuffed animal up to his ear. "What's that you say?" he asked the toy. "I think you should say it louder."

Billy giggled as Justin turned the stuffed animal toward him and began talking in a high-pitched voice.

"Woofy... woof... woof. I want to go home with you, Billy."

"You do?" Billy asked, surprised.

"Yes. Woof."

178

My son looked at me. "Can he, mommy? Pease?"

Laughing, I nodded. "Yes. How can I say 'no' to either of those faces?" I replied, meaning Justin's, too. He looked so sweet, trying to make Billy smile.

"Here you go," said Justin, handing him the stuffed animal.

"What's his name?" Billy asked, hugging it against his chest.

"He didn't say. I think you'd better come up with one," he replied.

"Tuffy. I'm naming him that because he's stwong. Wike you," said Billy, pointing at Justin's thick arms.

"Now *that* is a good name," said Justin, fluffing his curly hair. "Good choice, kiddo."

"Thanks."

"Who are the flowers for?" asked Joanna, also amused at watching the exchange between the rough-looking biker and my small son.

Justin looked at the flowers. "Oh, yeah. Sorry. These are for you," he said, holding them out to me.

"Thank you," I replied, staring up at him. The pain medicine they'd given me must have been doing some strange things, because I was actually happy to see him.

"You're welcome."

I grabbed the roses, brought them to my nose, and inhaled. It had been so long since I'd gotten flowers. "They're lovely."

He grinned.

Joanna cleared her throat.

"Um, this is my sister-in-law, Joanna. Joanna, this is Justin."

"Nice to meet you," he said, holding out his hand.

She shook it. "Nice to meet you," Joanna replied, a funny smile on her face. "Don't they also call you Tank?"

"Yes."

"You're the new gang leader," she said, nodding toward his cut.

"I'm the new club president," he corrected.

"Oh. Of course," said Joanna. "You probably don't remember me, but I defended one of your members a few years ago, when he was charged with arson. Stephen Fey."

"That's right. I recall a little bit about the case. It was a bogus charge, obviously."

"Oh, of course," she replied, smiling again. "And I got him off."

Justin's eyes twinkled. "Yeah, I do remember him talking about you getting him off."

Joanna's face turned bright red. "Is that right?"

He smiled. "He told all of us that it turned out to be a very happy ending."

I bit back a smile.

Laughing nervously, Joanna stood up. "Well, if you ever see him around, tell him I said hello."

"Will do," he replied.

Joanna tapped Billy on the shoulder. "How about we go and find something to eat? I bet you're hungry."

He looked up at her. "Can I get some ice cweam?"

"I don't know. Mom, what do you think?" she replied.

"I think that sounds like a great dessert to eat," I said. "*After* you eat some soup. The doctor said that it's pretty good here."

"I don't wike soup," said Billy, looking grumpy again. I knew he was exhausted and wondered what was taking the doctor so long.

"What are you talking about?" said Justin. He flexed his muscles. "If you want to grow big and strong, you have to eat lots of soup."

His eyes widened. "Soup made you gwow big muskles like that?"

"Yes. Soup has lots of vitamins and minerals. Especially chicken noodle," Justin said. "Which is my favorite."

Billy looked at Joanna. "I want chicken noodle soup."

I smiled. "I have a feeling they might offer that in the cafeteria."

She took his hand. "Good choice."

"Bye, Mommy," he said, looking over at me.

I waved. "Bye, sweetie."

A worried expression spread across his face.

"It's okay. I'm not going anywhere and Joanna will be with you," I reassured him.

Nodding, he allowed her to lead him out of the room.

Justin sat down next to me, in the chair. "That's quite a kid you've got there. How old is he?"

"He'll be three soon," I said, wondering why he was there.

"I can't believe what those assholes did to you. I heard about it from Raptor. Joanna told him all about it."

"I know. I'm just happy they didn't get away with it. If it wasn't for your guys, I don't know what might have happened."

"I'm glad they were able to help. Do you have any idea of where Phillip is?"

"All I know is that Betty called to warn him and then, of course, the police have been trying to get ahold of him."

"He's probably on the run," said Justin.

I nodded. "He caused a lot of heartache. Well, so did I." Our eyes met. I licked my lips. "I can't actually blame anyone for what I did, Justin, I'm so sorry." My eyes filled with tears again. "I feel so… disgusted with myself."

He grabbed my hand, surprising me. "I know you do, Raina. You don't have to say anything more about it."

"Yes, I do," I said, wiping my eyes with the back of my other hand. "I want you to know that after Phillip is caught and sentenced, I'm turning myself in for killing your father."

Justin frowned. "No. You don't have to do that."

"I broke the law and did something so despicable. I have to face the repercussions of what I've done."

"No. I won't let you."

I pulled my hand away from his. "You have no choice. This isn't up to you."

He pointed toward the doorway. "You have a son who has been through so much shit in the last couple of weeks, you can't dump more on him. He needs his mother. Christ, Raina, what's he going to do if you're in jail? Live with *Cole*?"

"I know what you're saying," I said, trying to keep my composure. The thought of leaving Billy was killing me. "But I need to do the right thing."

He leaned forward. "The right thing is to let this go. For your son."

"Can't you see, I'm doing this *for* my son? Someday he's going to find out what I did and I want him to know that I stepped forward and did the right thing afterward. I need to do this. "

He closed his eyes and groaned. "Woman, you are so damn

stubborn that you won't even listen to reason."

"Reason? I'm well beyond reason, so don't waste your breath," I replied, grabbing a tissue from the nightstand next to the bed. "Anyway, it's the decent thing to do and for once, I'm going to go that route."

"Decent? Come on, darlin'. You have got to be the most decent person I've ever met."

I laughed harshly. "I guess you really don't know me then."

"Bullshit. I know what I see. From looking at your son and seeing how much he loves you, I can tell that you are a caring and decent mother."

I laughed bitterly. "Right now, I feel like I'm some kind of joke. Trying to be a good mother to my son when I went and shot another son's father."

"You weren't in your right mind. You know that the defense lawyer I'd hire would get you off anyway. They would say it was a crime of passion. Temporary insanity."

I raised my eyebrows. "Did you just offer to pay for my attorney?" I asked incredulously.

"Yes. And... lady, I don't know about you, but I'd rather not spend thousands of dollars on an obvious outcome."

"How do you know what that would be?"

"Because I'm not going to testify against you. If I do or say anything, it would be speaking on your behalf."

Stunned, I didn't know what to say. I would have never have guessed that he'd take my side.

Justin went on. "So, whether you like it or not, you'll get off, and you should. Nobody is going to want to send a woman, who's been through so much, off to jail."

"But –"

"I'm not finished," he said firmly. "If you decide to do this, which is a damn mistake, the lawyers will ultimately get the case dropped and collect their big fat paychecks, which are all they really care about. Knowing this, I'd advise that you save all of us money, time, and anguish. Not to mention that your son doesn't have to ever find out about what happened."

"I don't see how he could *not* find out."

"Who's going to tell him? Not me. The cops don't know anything about it either."

"Cole knows," I replied.

"I can keep him quiet," he said, his lip twitching. "I'll slice off his tongue if he tries giving you up."

I snorted. "He'd never give me up."

"Maybe not to the cops, but he'll open up about it someday. Maybe to one of his club members. Or a guy at a bar."

"You don't know Cole. He only wants to protect me."

"If he's riding with those kinds of fuckers, then I know more about him than you probably do."

I sighed. "To be honest, I was hoping to talk him out of joining their club."

"If you don't, he's going to end up dead one day, and," he raised his hands in the air, "I'm not threatening him by no means. The Devil's Rangers have a lot of enemies. Joining their club is like playing Russian Roulette. One day the gun is going to go off and it's going to be messy."

I frowned.

"Speaking of your brother, have you spoken to him lately?"

"No. I suppose I should call him," I said, looking toward my purse. "And my Uncle Sal."

"I took the liberty of contacting Sal. He was worried sick about you."

I stared at him in surprise. "Thank you. Did you tell him about Billy?"

"No. I thought you'd want to."

"I do, actually. He's not going to believe it. I still can't myself."

"I'm sure life seems like a total mind-fuck for you right now. At least that trip is ending well."

I snorted. "No shit."

"By the way, how are you getting back to Davenport?"

"Joanna's going to drive me. We'll be leaving soon."

"I'll follow you back. Make sure nothing else happens to you guys."

"You don't have to do that."

"I know, but I want to."

"Why are you being so nice to me?" I asked, wondering if it was because of Cole.

TWENTY NINE

TANK

I WASN'T REALLY SURE myself. All I knew is that I had this wanting to protect the young woman in front of me, along with her son. Sure, she was gorgeous, with those arctic blue eyes and full lips. Not to mention that she was still wearing a hospital gown and I could tell that she wasn't wearing a bra. Chances were, she wasn't wearing any panties either. I was such a sick bastard. "Someone has to."

She looked disappointed as if expecting something more. "Oh."

"And I was really hoping to get into your panties before Billy and Joanna returned. Or should I say, under that hospital gown."

Raina's jaw dropped.

I laughed at the shock on her face. "Just playing, princess. Trying to lighten the mood. It's been a hell of day, hasn't it?"

Raina gave me a slow, sexy smile. "Damn right and it could turn out to be a hell of a night if you play your cards right."

My eyebrows shot up. "Uh... what?" I asked, not sure if I'd heard her correctly.

"Go and lock the door."

I stood up. "Seriously?"

She began to laugh.

"That's cold," I said, shaking my head.

"Sorry. I just had to fuck with you. You should have seen your face."

I wondered if she'd noticed the reaction below my belt. "I'm a horn-dog, what can I say?" I replied while nonchalantly trying to adjust myself. "Have to admit, I thought you were offering me a bone and I was about ready to run with it."

"And I thought it was you, offering me a bone."

I grinned. "I'm always offering that. I just need to be a gentleman right now before you find out what I'm really about and kick me out of here."

"And what are you really about?"

"What do you think I'm really about?"

"Personally, I think you're just a softy who would do almost anything for a woman."

"You've got that backward. See, when I'm hard women will do almost anything for *me*."

She laughed and shook her head.

"You think I'm joking? They don't call me Tank for nothing."

"I figured it had something to do with you eating a lot."

Grinning wickedly, I dropped my eyes to her lap. "I do have a hearty appetite."

Raina's cheeks turned pink.

"Sorry. Too much?"

"No. I work in a bar. I've seen and heard it all."

I work in a bar, too. Fortunately, in the back."

"What do you mean?"

"I own Griffin's. I spend most of my time in the office, going over the books and shit."

"Ah. Running a strip joint must be a lot of work."

I shrugged. "It's not so bad. I helped my old man out for many years, and learned a few things. The club has helped out a lot, too."

"That's good. You seem like the kind of guy people really want to help."

"Probably because I'm intimidating."

She could tell I was joking and smiled. "I have no doubt you are when you need to be. But, I also see a really good guy. And... you seem to be pretty sweet with kids, too."

"It's easy to do when you don't have to live with them."

"So, you don't want children?"

"What do you mean? I have seventeen of them already."

Raina gave me a shocked look. "What?"

"The guys in my club. They're just a bunch of kids. Can't see myself taking care of more than those rascals."

She smiled.

There was a knock on the door and the doctor, an older man with gray hair and glasses, entered the room. He looked at me and then Raina. "I bet you're ready to get out of here. Is this your ride?"

"No," she said laughing. "He's just a friend."

I stood up and held out my hand. "The name's Tank. How's she doing, Doc?"

Sliding the clipboard under his arm, he shook my hand. "She's doing well. Raina was a very lucky woman."

"Good to hear." I looked at her. "I'll let you talk to the doctor while I go find Billy and Joanna."

"Thanks," she said.

"Nice meeting you, Doc."

"Same to you," he said.

As I was leaving the room, I overheard him asking her about insurance and stopped outside the door.

"I don't have any right now," she said in a low voice. "Can I set up some kind of a payment plan?"

"I'm sure the hospital can arrange that."

"Thanks goodness," she replied. "I'm a little strapped for cash."

"Don't worry about medical bills right now," he said in a kind voice. "Worry about recovering and taking care of your son."

"I'll try."

Wanting to make things easier for her so she could focus on more important things, I headed toward the front desk and made arrangements to pay her medical bills.

THIRTY

RAINA

I T WAS ALMOST ten by the time we left the hospital. Billy had since fallen asleep and Justin carried him out to my car, while Joanna pushed me in a wheelchair.

"Darn, we don't have a car seat," I said, remembering how I'd taken it out of the car the week before.

"Let's get one then," said Tank. "There's a store right up the road."

"Good idea. We'll just have to use a seatbelt until we get there," said Joanna, in a low voice. "I'm sure he'll be fine, but if we get pulled over, I never said that."

"Right," I said, pulling myself out of the wheelchair. I opened the back door of the car and watched as Justin gently put Billy inside and buckled the seatbelt.

Billy, who was groggy, opened his eyes. "Where's Tuffy?"

"Here he is," I replied, holding him up.

Justin took the stuffed animal from me and handed it to Billy, who wrapped his arms around the toy and smiled.

"Thank you," I whispered, smiling warmly at him.

He grinned back at me through the darkness. "My pleasure. He's a good kid."

"Bye, Tank," said Billy, yawning. "I wuv you."

The look on Justin's face was priceless. I knew he didn't know Billy enough to actually have real feelings for him, but that didn't stop the burly biker from trying his best to return the sentiment.

"You know, kid, you're pretty easy to love yourself," he replied.

Joanna looked at me over the car, smiling in amusement. I grinned back.

"You really don't have to come with us," I told him as he closed the back door.

"Nonsense," he replied. "I said we'd get this kid a car seat and that's what we're going to do."

"I can do it myself," I said, feeling a little awkward that he was doing so much for us.

Joanna cleared her throat and opened the driver's side door. "Yeah... I'll be waiting in the car," she said. "While you two figure things out."

"Nothing to figure out," said Justin, starting to walk away toward his bike, which was on the other side of the parking lot. "The store is right up the road. You can see it from here. I'll meet you there."

"If that's what you really want," I said. "To go shopping for car seats."

He turned around and began walking backward. "Let's be real, here. You already know what I want," he said, a smile in his voice. "And just so you know... I always get what I want."

Understanding his meaning, I felt a tingling in a region that had been dormant for the last twelve months.

"I don't know what that means," I lied.

"Don't worry. You'll learn soon enough."

I opened my mouth to give him a witty comeback, but nothing came out. The truth was, I didn't exactly know how to respond.

"Cat got your tongue?"

"Something like that."

He gave me a wicked grin and headed to his motorcycle.

When I got into the car, Joanna gave me a strange look.

"What?" I asked.

"What's going on with you two?" she asked, starting the engine.

"I don't really know," I replied, buckling my seatbelt. "We just met yesterday."

She backed out of the parking spot and we both watched as Justin swung his leg over the side of the motorcycle and started the engine.

"Mm… He's gorgeous, I'll give him that. But, he's also dangerous."

"I know," I replied. "I'm not getting involved with him, if that's what you're wondering."

"Good, because you already have enough things to worry about in your life at the moment. Hell, so do I," she mumbled.

"Speaking of which, do you know if they caught Phillip yet?" I asked, glancing toward the backseat. Billy had already fallen back asleep, still holding the stuffed animal.

"No. I haven't heard anything. I'm sure they'll find him pretty quickly, though."

"If not, you should stay at my place," I said. "In case he shows up at yours."

"As much as I appreciate your offer, my mother has already insisted that I stay with her. You're more than welcome to join me, too. At least until things get settled down?"

"Thank you, but I just want to bring Billy home, where he belongs. I think he needs to be there, especially after what's been happening."

She nodded. "You're probably right. He needs to get back to his routine and the comfort of his bed."

I pulled my phone out of my purse. "I'm surprised that Cole

hasn't called me back, yet," I said, a little worried.

"Did you leave him a message about finding Billy?"

"Yes, and that's why I'm a little freaked out that he hasn't responded. Not even a text."

She bit her lip. "Hopefully, he's okay. I still don't understand what the big hype is about joining that club of his. Tank's club is bad enough. I've heard the stories around town. But, the Devil's Rangers? Those guys are nothing but criminals. How did he get involved with them anyway?"

"A friend of his from high school got him into it," I said. "He started hanging around the club and then they made him a Prospect. I hope he's okay."

"Well, he's a grown man and I hate to say it, but you and Billy would be better off not having him around."

"He's my brother," I said.

"He's also a brother to thugs and that puts you and Billy in danger."

I sighed. "I know. I just wish I could talk some sense into him."

"I know. He's going to either learn the hard way, of who he's mixed up with, or... I don't even want to think about it."

Neither did I, but I knew she was right.

We followed Justin to the large warehouse store and parked next to him. He got off of his bike and walked over.

I opened up the door and was about to get out when he stopped me.

"You shouldn't be walking on that leg. Why don't you stay out here and I'll run in and buy him a car seat?"

"No. You don't have to do that," I insisted.

"I know but I'm going to anyway."

"I'll go and buy him one," said Joanna, opening up her door.

"No. I said that I'd handle this," said Justin. "Just stay out here and watch over these two."

Joanna frowned. "You sure?"

"Of course I'm sure. Do you have any preference in car seats?" he asked me.

"Something safe but not too expensive," I replied.

He nodded. "Okay. I'll be back."

"Thank you!" I called, as he turned around and began walking toward the store entrance.

He waved his hand in answer.

Joanna got back into the vehicle and we watched him strut into the store.

"I swear to God, that man has the nicest ass I've ever seen," she said under her breath.

I'd been checking it out too. "Yes, it's… very nice."

"If he ever needs a lawyer, you let me know. I'll let him pay off my retainer in bed," she said, pulling down the car's visor.

"I thought you said he was too dangerous to get involved with?" I said, smirking.

"I'm not talking about getting involved. I'm just talking about an hour on his lap," she whispered. "Maybe a little 'me' time on his face, too."

Biting back laughter, I turned around to make sure that Billy hadn't heard. Luckily, he was still sleeping. "How can you be thinking about *that*, after everything that's happened?" I asked, although my own mind had been going 'there' as well. Especially with Justin. There was something about him that was beginning to get under my skin.

She let out a sigh. "To be honest, we haven't been intimate for so long and the man has been so hard to live with. I told you that."

"Yes. Why did you stay married to him then?" I asked.

She shrugged. "I don't know. I guess I thought things would get better and decided to wait."

"It's a good thing you did, otherwise we might not have known that Billy was still alive."

"Very true," she said, yawning.

"Are you going to be okay to drive? You must be exhausted."

"I have to admit, I'm bushed. It's only a two hour drive, though. I should be fine."

As much as I wanted to go home that night, she looked wiped out and with the pain medication I was taking, I didn't want to risk driving. "Maybe we should get a motel room? Just for the night?" I said. "What do you think?"

She yawned again. "You know, that might not be a bad idea. I'm not looking forward to facing my mother tonight, either. She's going to barrage me with questions about Phillip, you, and Billy. Speaking of motels, look," she pointed up the street to a sign that read 'Vacancy'. "There's one right there."

I turned to look. "I think we should do it."

"Are you sure? Billy made his demands pretty clear. He wants to go home."

"I know, but he can go home tomorrow. What's important is

that Billy is back with me. And, besides, he's got Tuffy," I replied, smiling again.

She sat up straighter, her eyes glittering in the darkness. "Okay, you know what? If we are staying out here, it's going to be my treat and I say we find an actual 'hotel' with a nice restaurant and maybe even a masseuse." She pulled out her cell phone. "After everything that's happened, I'd like some R&R. Even if it's for only one night."

My eyes widened. "Really?"

"Yes," she replied, searching the internet.

"I'd just like a few hours to sleep," I said, sitting deeper into the seat. "Maybe a burger, too. I can't remember the last time I ate."

"We'll get one of those for you, too. Oh, here we go..." she smiled. "The James Drake Hotel. They even have a spa." Her smile faltered. "It's not open right now, though. Drat."

"The hotel?"

"No. The spa. I want a massage, dammit."

"Maybe you can talk him into it," I said, watching as Justin stepped out of the store carrying a big box.

"Honey, if anyone is getting a massage from that guy, it's going to be you."

THIRTY ONE

TANK

AFTER SPENDING TWO-HUNDRED bucks on a car seat, I was reminded that children were not cheap. Billy was worth it, though, and that's why I bought one of the sturdier models.

As I stepped out of the store and back toward Raina and her sister-in-law, I noticed both of them staring at me with silly grins on their faces.

"What's so funny?" I asked.

"Nothing," they both said in unison and then looked away.

I walked around the car, to Raina's side, and put the box down on the asphalt. "Will this work?"

She opened up the door and stood up slowly. "Yes. You didn't have to get him that model. I know how much those ones cost," she said, frowning.

"You can't put a value on that little guy's life," I said. "He's worth it."

"I know he is but we have another one in my garage," she said. "This one is really just to get us back into town."

I tore open the box. "Then he'll get back safely."

"I can't pay you back for this," she said.

"Did I ask you to?" I asked, pulling out the car-seat.

"No, but –"

"Then don't worry about it," I said. "Hell, this thing is pretty sturdy. Maybe I'll just strap it to my bike and teach him how to ride."

She snorted. "Right."

"Problem is, I don't think the make brain buckets in his size. I'll just keep the car seat in my truck at home so when we go out, he can join us."

"When we go out?" she repeated, watching as I pulled the plastic off of the chair.

I smirked. "If you prefer something quiet, you can cook me dinner at your place."

"I don't think that would be a good idea," she said, lowering her voice.

"Open the door for me, will you, princess?" I replied, ignoring the comment.

"Oh, we're back to princess again, huh?" she said, doing what I asked.

I leaned down and put the car seat into the backseat, next to Billy. Then I touched his arm. "Hey, buddy," I said in a low voice. "We got you something."

Billy's long eyelashes fluttered open and when he noticed me, a big smile spread across his face. "You're still hewe?"

"I sure am. Check this out," I said, patting the car seat. "I think it has its own shocks and airbags."

Without saying anything, he unbuckled his seatbelt and climbed into the chair.

"You like it?" I asked, adjusting the straps to make sure they weren't too loose or tight.

He nodded.

"Good." I buckled him into the chair, handed him his stuffed dog, and stood back up. "That should work, huh?" I asked, turning to look at Raina.

She was smiling at me again. "Yes. Definitely. Thank you."

"You're welcome," I replied, pulling my key out of my jeans.

"So, we ready to hit it?"

"Actually, we're going to stay at a hotel tonight. One here in town," said Joanna, through the window.

I stared at them in surprise. "You're not going back to Davenport tonight?"

"No," said Raina. We're both too tired to drive and decided that it would be better to get a room here in town."

I rubbed my chin. "Okay. That works for me."

"Thanks again for everything," Raina replied. "You and your club have been great."

"You're welcome," I answered. "I'm just glad everyone is safe."

"Me, too," she said.

"Stay safe," said Joanna, starting up the engine to the car again.

"Where are we going?" I asked, enjoying the look of surprise on both women's faces. Obviously, they thought I'd head out. I'd already made a decision that I'd be sticking on Raina like glue. I still wanted to talk to her brother and something in my gut told me that she needed someone to watch over her. At least until the cops caught Phillip. If they didn't, I'd pull some strings and try to make it happen.

"You're not going back home tonight?" Raina asked.

"Nah. I could use some rest and a bite to eat," I answered.

"I just made reservations at the James Drake Hotel," said Joanna.

"Okay. Let's go," I said. "I'll follow you if you know where it is."

"I do now. I'm not sure if they have any more rooms available," said Joanna. "You might want to call."

"I'll take my chances," I replied, walking toward my bike.

She said something to Raina and both women giggled again.

I turned around. "Okay, I give up – is there something on the back of my jeans? Every time I turn around, you two start laughing."

"It's more what's in your jeans," said Joanna, biting her lower lip.

"Oh, my God," said Raina, putting a hand over her face in horror.

I smiled. "Oh, yeah?"

From Joanna's expression, it was obvious she hadn't meant to say those words out loud. "I'll take my foot out of my mouth and use it to drive now," she said quickly, her face red.

"We'll meet you there," said Raina, getting into the car. She winced and mumbled something.

I swung my leg over the bike. "You okay?"

She looked at me, smiling grimly. "It hurts, but I'll live."

"You sure you don't want a ride on my bike?" I asked, starting my engine.

Her eyes glittered as she looked at my Harley. "Probably not a good idea."

"Another time?"

"Maybe."

"I'll take that as a 'yes'."

"Somehow that doesn't surprise me," she answered, smirking.

"It shouldn't. Like I said – I always get my way."

"You must have been an only-child," she said, getting ready to swing the door closed.

"Good call, but that's not why."

She raised her eyebrow.

I looked down at my lap.

"The bike?"

I smiled wickedly "The ride."

Raina looked confused when she shut the door. As she put her seatbelt on, I saw a smile creep up onto her face.

THIRTY TWO

RAINA

WHEN WE ARRIVED at the hotel, shortly before eleven, we found that there were no other rooms available.

"That's okay, Raina and Billy can stay with me," said Joanna. "Tank, you can have the other room."

"Are you sure?" I asked.

"Of course. My room has two queen-sized beds." That's plenty of room for us." She looked over my shoulder at Justin and smiled. "You can take the room with the king."

"Thanks," he said, pulling out his credit card. He handed it to the hotel concierge "Charge them to this card."

"You don't have to do that," said Joanna, frowning. "I've already used my VISA to reserve the rooms."

He shrugged. "That's fine. They can switch the credit cards."

"Is this what you want to do?" the hotel attendant asked Joanna.

"Yes, this is what she wants to do," said Justin, holding the card in front of the woman's face.

Joanna sighed. "Fine. Whatever. It's your call and I'm beginning to see that arguing with you is a waste of time."

"Now you're learning," said Justin, as the girl ran his card through the machine.

Billy tugged on my hand. "I want to stay with Tank. Pwease, mommy?"

"No, honey. You have to stay with me and Joanna."

Billy was about to protest when Justin leaned down on his knee. "As much as I'd love to have you with me, you gotta stay with your momma and make sure she takes care of that leg of hers."

He tiled his head. "I do?"

Justin nodded. "Yep. She shouldn't be walking on it too much and you gotta stay on her about that. Maybe even get her a glass of water when she needs it... or turn off the television if she asks."

"Why can't Aunt Joanna do dat?"

"Because she's tuckered. She's going to fall asleep and someone needs to be in charge. That person is you."

His eyes widened. "Me?"

"You're the man of the house now, aren't you?"

He bobbed his head up and down.

Justin squeezed his shoulder. "That's what I thought. So, you make sure your momma takes it easy and if you gotta scold her, you do that."

"Okay," he said, looking almost exuberant at that idea.

Justin laughed and stood up. "Looks like I don't have to worry about you tonight."

"Guess not," I replied, wondering why he was so worried about me anyway.

"NOW, ISN'T THIS better than a cheap motel room?" asked Joanna, walking out of the bathroom wearing a white hotel robe. She'd just gotten done taking a shower and Billy had crashed after the three of us shared a pizza.

I looked around the room. It wasn't a suite, but it was large, spacious, and clean. The mattresses were luxurious, however, and totally worth the extra money.

"It's nice, I agreed.

"Wonder how that biker is doing in the next room?" she mused, pouring some of the hotel's lotion into the palm of her hand. She began rubbing it on her leg. "He's been very quiet over there."

"To be honest, I don't think he's there right now." Justin had mentioned that he was going to grab a bite to eat in the bar before we'd ordered food ourselves. He'd invited me to join him, but I'd declined, not wanting to leave Billy out of my sight.

Her eyebrows shot up. "Where do you think he went?"

"He mentioned grabbing a bite downstairs."

"I should have joined him. I could use a tall glass of wine after everything we saw tonight."

"You could still go down there," I said.

"Nah," she said, rubbing more lotion onto her other leg. She tilted her head and smiled. "By now, he's probably sitting with some pretty little thing, having a cocktail. In another hour or so, we'll probably hear some noises going on in the next room that will make you regret not joining him yourself."

"I'm not looking for..." I looked at Billy and lowered my voice, "anything other than friendship with Justin."

"That's not what your eyes say every time you look at the man."

"I'm just grateful for everything he's done. There's nothing more."

"You don't have to give me any excuses. Heck, if I were you, though, I'd thank him the way a man like that wants to be thanked. With a blow-job or good old-fashioned sex," she whispered, grinning wickedly. "I'm thinking that he'd be open to either."

"Like I'm in the position to skip off and do either of those things," I said, waving toward my son and then my leg.

"I'll watch Billy," she said, putting the cap back onto the lotion. "And you're not running a marathon. All you have to do is lie there and enjoy yourself," she whispered.

An image of me lying underneath a man like Justin made my sex tighten. I imagined wrapping my legs around his hard, tattooed body and opening myself up to him. From the bulge in his jeans, he had a lot to offer a woman, especially one who hadn't had sex in ages. And he did brag that he knew how to give a good ride. "No. It's not going to happen."

"Suit yourself. I'd keep his number handy, though. You'll regret it if you don't."

"I thought you said I shouldn't get involved with a guy like him?" I reminded her again.

"Who said anything about getting involved? I'm talking about having yourself some fun. After the last few weeks, you certainly deserve it."

I sighed. Even if I wanted to have sex, I didn't think I could look Justin in the eye when we were curled up in bed together. As much as he claimed to not blame me for killing Slammer, I still blamed myself. "I think I'm going to take a shower," I said. Maybe even a cold one after some of the thoughts that had been running through my mind.

"Careful with your bandage," she said, nodding toward my leg.

"I know. They gave me a couple of other bandages along with some extra ointment," I replied. "It's really not as bad as I thought it was, though."

"That's good."

I nodded and looked down at Billy again. "I gave him some of that medicine for his ear. It's in the mini-refrigerator. Remind me not to forget that stuff tomorrow."

"I'll write myself a note," she said, walking over to the other bed. "By the way, there's another robe in the bathroom."

"Thanks," I said, hobbling toward it.

TRYING NOT TO get the bandage wet in the shower proved to be more challenging than I'd thought. Ultimately, I removed the damn thing and bore through all of the unpleasantness.

When I was finished, I dried myself, put the robe on, which stopped just above my knees, and then went in search of the ointment and bandages.

The lights were out and both Billy and Joanna were sound asleep when I stepped out of the bathroom. Trying not to run into a wall, I grabbed the bag of medical supplies the doctor had given me and snuck back into the bathroom. Inside of the bag, I found the bandages, but the ointment was missing.

"Shit," I mumbled, recalling that I'd given Justin the tube to hold for me right before he'd carried Billy to the car. Sighing, I looked down at my thigh again, which was tender, and decided that I needed more of it. Making sure that the robe was cinched tightly around my waist, I quietly left the room and stepped next door, to Justin's. Before I could knock, however, I heard noises coming out of his room. Thinking they were rather strange, I pressed my ear against the door.

"Yes," gasped a woman's voice. "Right there… uh, huh!"

Shocked, I jumped back.

"Hey," said a voice down the hallway.

My head whipped around and there was Justin, walking toward me with a bucket of ice.

I stared at him in confusion. "I… who's in your room?"

"Nobody. At least… I hope not," he said, walking a little faster.

"I heard a woman's voice," I replied.

Frowning, he took out his room key and slid it into the door. The light turned green and he pushed it open. "Oh," he said, stopping abruptly in the doorway.

I got on my tippy toes and peered over his shoulder. There wasn't anyone in the room, but the television was playing a porno.

Justin walked over to the bed and grabbed the remote. He switched off the television. "Sorry about that. I don't know why that was playing."

I smirked. "So, that wasn't your choice?"

"No. Hell no. It must have just started playing on its own. To be honest, I would have chosen something much dirtier," he said, flashing me a wicked grin.

"I'm not even going to ask," I said, feeling my face heat up. "Anyway, the reason I'm here is because I think you still have that ointment the doctor gave me. For my leg?"

His yes traveled down my robe. "Oh, yeah. Sorry. How does it feel?" he asked digging into the front pocket of his jeans.

"I took a shower, obviously," I said, pointing to my wet hair.

"And the bandage came off. It's definitely sore."

"Can I see it?" he asked, looking at where the robe was tied around my waist. From the look in his eyes, he might have been talking about something else.

"My wound?"

"Unless there's something else you'd rather show me," he said, grinning again.

"I doubt you want to see the wound," I said, quickly, changing the subject. "It's gross."

"Somehow I doubt anything on you would be gross. Come here," he said, grabbing my hand.

"I should probably get back to my room," I said, allowing him to lead me over to the bed like a puppy-dog.

"You can. Afterward. Sit down."

Not knowing what else to do, I did what he asked and sat down on the bed.

"I'll be right back," he said, setting the ice bucket down. He then went into the bathroom and washed his hands.

Feeling jittery, I stood back up. "I should really get back to my own room," I called out. "Billy is going to wonder where I'm at if he wakes up."

Drying his hands, Justin stepped out of the bathroom and walked back over to me. "He's sleeping?"

"For now."

"You'd probably wake him up if you go over there now, so park your ass back down and relax. I just want to have a look at your wound. Make sure the doctor did a good job with the stitches."

213

"Of course he did a good job," I said.

"I'll be the judge of that. Sit."

Not knowing what else to do, I sat down on the edge of the bed.

Justin got down on his knees and began taking the cover off of the ointment. "I'll let you show me where it is."

Swallowing, I leaned to the side and pulled my robe up. The gash from the bullet was on the outside of my hip.

"Jesus," he said, staring at my leg.

I moved my leg a little and looked down at it. "I know. It's gross. I warned you."

Licking his lips, his eyes met mine. "I'm going to try something new and be a gentleman for once."

"Well that's a relief," I said jokingly.

He pulled my robe down, covering up a spot that had peeked through unknowingly.

My face turned red. "Did I just... flash you?"

"Let's just say that I know you're not wearing panties," he said with a wicked smile.

THIRTY THREE

TANK

I T TOOK EVERY ounce of restraint to not rip open her robe and bury my face between those creamy, pale legs. Especially, now that she was looking at me the way she was.

"Oh," she whispered. "I'm sorry."

"Don't be," I answered, staring up into her blue eyes. "It was a nice view."

She lowered her lashes and blushed.

"Let's get this over with before I do something stupid and you slap me."

"Maybe I wouldn't."

I looked back up at her in surprise.

An invitation?

"Wouldn't what?" I asked. I was so hard, I could barely breathe and the electricity in the room seemed to amplify everything. Including the pulsating of my cock, which was straining to get out of my jeans.

She just smiled.

"Don't be teasing me like that," I said, placing my hand on her leg. It was smooth and I could smell whatever soap she'd used in the shower. It smelled almost like honeysuckle.

Raina let out a ragged breath. "Sorry. You'd better put that ointment on."

I removed my hand and squirted the ointment onto my index finger. Then I very gently, rubbed it on and around her wound.

"Ah," she said, sucking in her breath. "Damn, that hurts."

"Sorry. You have another bandage to put over it?" I asked,

wiping my finger off on the side of my jeans.

She reached into her robe and pulled one out. As she moved, the fabric slipped again and I caught another glimpse of her muff.

"Let me have that," I said, grabbing it from her. I needed to do something with my hands before they did something to her. I ripped off the plastic and carefully put it over the wound.

"Thanks," she said, staring at me.

My eyes dipped to the belt on her robe again. "You're welcome."

"I should go," she said, pulling the fabric down over her thighs.

I stood up and turned around with my raging hard-on. "Or, you could stay and have a drink," I said, heading toward the bucket of ice. "I was just about to have a nightcap."

"Okay," she said quickly.

Surprised, I turned to look at her. "Really?"

"Sure, what do you have?"

"Just what's in the mini bar," I said, walking over to the refrigerator. I knelt down. "Looks like we have vodka, rum, oh... there are a couple bottles of wine, too,"

"What kind?" she asked, walking over to stand next to me.

I held out the two bottles. "A Merlot and a White Zinfandel."

She leaned down to look, giving me an up-close and personal view of her cleavage.

"I'll take the White Zin," she said, standing back up. "But, just one bottle."

"They're only five ounces," I said, standing up, too. "Two won't kill you."

She smirked. "Are you trying to get me drunk?"

I wasn't sure what I was trying to do, but I knew one thing. I didn't want her to leave. "I'm just trying to help you relax," I said, staring down at her.

She took one of the bottles out of my hand, opened it up, and drank it down like water.

"What are you doing?"

She dropped the bottle into the pocket of her robe. "Trying to get the nerve up."

"For what?"

"To thank you. Properly."

THIRTY FOUR

RAINA

*P*ROPERLY?"

"Yes," I said, feeling the wine begin to warm me. I thought about what Joanna had said and knew what I had to do. What I needed to do.

He stood there, staring at me curiously.

I took a deep breath and then slid my arms around his neck.

His eyes began to smolder. "Fuck me," he whispered in surprise.

I got on my tippy toes and pulled his mouth to mine. At first, Justin stiffened up, like he wasn't sure how to react. But then, his hand was in my hair and he was kissing me back.

I arched my back and moaned in delight when I felt his hands slip under my robe to my ass, squeezing so hard it was almost painful.

"Damn, princess," he gasped, leaving my lips for a second to catch his breath. "I did *not* see that coming."

Before I could answer, he came back for more, taking my breath away with his kisses. Then his lips moved down my neck, inching his way to the swell of my breasts, his hot tongue giving me cold shivers.

"Should we really do this?" I whispered.

"We already are," he said, pulling the belt off of my robe. It opened up and he stared down at my body. "Even better than I imagined. You're beautiful, Raina."

"You're not so bad yourself," I said, sliding my other hand under his leather cut and over his muscles.

Justin cupped my breasts and raised the right one to his mouth. My legs turned to jelly as he licked and sucked on the nipple, teasing my nub with his tongue. I threw my head back and moaned in delight

221

as he moved to the other one. Hornier than all hell, I slid my hand down to his jeans and began stroking the thick outline of his cock.

He closed his eyes and groaned.

Aching for more, I unbuttoned Justin's fly, shoved his underwear to the side, and wrapped my hand around the mighty girth of his manhood. I'd never seen anything like it.

"Fuck me," he gasped, as I began moving my hand, up and down the shaft. Hot, hard, and pulsating, I knew there was no way I'd leave tonight without feeling it inside of me.

"No, fuck me," I purred, rubbing the moist pre-cum with my thumb.

Tightening his jaw, he picked me up in his arms and brought me over to the bed. Setting me down, he pushed my robe away from my shoulders and then stood back up. He removed his cut and then pulled his jeans and underwear off.

"So, you definitely work out," I said, staring hungrily at his muscular body.

He crawled on top of me and buried his face into my neck. "I try," he whispered, kissing an area below my ear.

I closed my eyes as he began making a trail down my body with his warm, delicious tongue. As he moved farther south, I felt his fingers slide down to my sex.

"Damn, darlin', you're so wet," he said, rubbing my labia.

I moaned and pushed against his hand as his fingers worked me into a frenzy. Soon his lips took over and I gasped in pleasure as he began licking and sucking my clit.

"Fuck yes," I whispered, clutching the sheets tightly.

Justin pulled my thighs over his shoulders and continued

pleasuring me until the dam broke and my hips were bucking and I was screaming out his name in ecstasy.

Wiping his mouth with the back of his hand, he got off the bed, grabbed his wallet, and pulled out a condom. Slipping it on, he crawled on top of me.

THIRTY FIVE

TANK

I STARED DOWN AT Raina, knowing that I wasn't going to last. She was sexier than hell, with her round breasts and tight little pussy. I leaned down, capturing her mouth with mine. She wrapped her legs around my waist and I positioned myself at her opening. Grabbing her hips, I pushed into a wet tightness that grappled my cock like it was checking my blood pressure.

"Fuck," I growled.

"Oh, God, that feels good," she whispered.

Pulling out again, I plunged back in.

"Yes," she gasped, digging her nails into my back.

Groaning, I began fucking her faster and almost came when she began rubbing her clit.

"That's it, baby. Come for me again," I said, grabbing her breast. I leaned over and sucked her nipple and then went to the other one.

Raina's moans became louder with every thrust. Clenching my jaw, I kept going until she wailed out another orgasm. It sent me over the edge and I stiffened up as my cock exploded inside of her. When I was completely spent, I collapsed on top of her.

"Justin," she wheezed. "You're too heavy."

"Shit. I'm sorry," I replied, flipping off of her. I grabbed her hand and slipped my fingers through hers.

"That was nice," she said, a smile in her voice.

I turned to my side and looked down at her. "Nice? It was *nice*?!"

She chuckled. "Okay, it was fucking mind-blowing. You are the best piece of ass I've ever had. Is that better?"

"It's a start," I said, getting out of the bed. I walked into the bathroom and tossed the condom. "I'm hungry again. What about you?"

"I had pizza earlier," Raina called back.

Pizza sounded good. I decided to order one for myself. I'd had an order of buffalo wings in the restaurant earlier and a burger, but sex always made me hungry. "That's right. I think I'm going to order room-service."

"Order from Papa Tony's. That's what we had and it was delicious."

"Will do." I walked back into the other room and saw that she was slipping the robe back on. "What are you doing?"

She looked at me over her shoulder. "Getting dressed."

"Yeah, I noticed. Are you leaving?"

"I should really get back to my room. Check on Billy."

"Yeah. I understand." I grabbed my clothes and started getting dressed, too. "You guys will join me for breakfast tomorrow, though, right?"

"Sure. If that's what you want."

I pulled my jeans up. "Of course, I *want*. I also want you to stay here tonight. In my room."

"You know I can't."

"I know. I'm just telling you it's what I want. So you don't think that what happened here was just a..." My voice trailed off as I tried thinking of the right word.

She swung her hair over her shoulder and looked at me curiously. "A what?"

Truthfully, I wasn't sure what it was. I only knew that I wanted it to happen again. There was something about her that I wasn't ready to give up. "That it wasn't just a hook-up or something to pass the time."

"Oh."

"Oh?" I raised my eyebrow. She almost looked disappointed.

"To be honest, Justin, I don't think this *can* happen again."

THIRTY SIX

RAINA

I COULD TELL BY the look on his face that he hadn't been expecting me to blow him off.

"It's nothing to do with you," I went on. "Not personally."

Still, he said nothing.

"I mean, this was amazing and you seem like a really great guy. It's just that… I can't got out with anyone belonging to a motorcycle club. Your world is just too dangerous. It's obviously been proven, especially in the last few weeks."

"I feel you," he said. "You're worried about your son. I say we skip the dates and just sleep together."

I laughed. "Right."

"I'm serious," he said. "You're a single parent. You have a job and other priorities. I'm sure you work your ass off to raise that kid. I'm busy running both my club and Griffin's shit can be pretty stressful at times. Truth is… we both need an outlet to let off some steam."

"So, I'd be an outlet," I replied, amused.

"Not just you. We'd both be."

I stared at him in disbelief. "So, you're talking strictly sex? I'm pretty sure you can get that from half a dozen women at any given time. Especially being a club president."

He walked over to me. "Yeah, I can. But, here's the thing – they're not you."

I looked up at him. Damn, he was handsome. "And what's so special about me?"

"More than you realize, it looks like." He pulled me into his arms and kissed me hard. When he let me go, I was breathless and

229

dizzy. "Now, tell me you're willing to give that up?"

"It's not that I want to. Your world is dangerous. You have a lot of enemies. I can't take any chances. Not when I have a young son to raise."

"If that's what you're worried about, my club would protect you and Billy."

Like his club protected Slammer from me?

"Let me think about it." I could tell Justin was ready to argue this with me until I eventually caved in. I decided it would be easier to just ignore his calls.

His face relaxed. "Okay."

"I'm going back to my room. I'll see you around eleven, in the lobby?"

Justin grabbed my ass. "Definitely. Unless you'd like to slip back here earlier and go for round two?"

I forced a laugh. "I think I need time to heal. I'm a little sore."

"Sorry," he said, with a pleased look on his face.

"I'm not. I wasn't lying when I said it was amazing," I said staring up at him.

He smiled arrogantly. "I know."

We kissed again and then I went back to my room. Fortunately, Billy and Joanna were still asleep and didn't wake up when I entered the room. Yawning, I got in bed, next to my son, and for the first time in quite a while, fell asleep without needing a drink.

THIRTY SEVEN

TANK

I WOKE UP, SEVERAL hours later to the sound of my phone ringing.

"What's up, Raptor?" I mumbled, looking over at the clock. It was almost ten a.m.

"You sleeping?"

"Not anymore."

"Sorry, man. I've been up for hours. Had to bring Sammy to daycare this morning."

I sat up and rubbed my face. "Explains why you're so fucking perky."

"I'm *perky* because I got an early morning piece of Adriana. That doesn't happen too often."

"Lucky you."

"You sound like you could use a mid-morning piece yourself, grump-ass."

I stared down at my morning wood. "No kidding. Had me something very nice last night," I said, smiling to myself.

"Really? Who?"

"None of your business."

"Since when, brother? You're always bragging about who you've been banging."

"Yeah, I know. This one doesn't want anyone to know."

"And you're agreeing to keep your mouth shut? What are you, in love?"

I laughed coldly. "I'm in love with fucking her again and it won't happen if I start telling the world."

"You don't have to tell the world. Just your best friend."

233

"Why the fuck you care so much?"

"Because this isn't like you."

"Maybe I'm turning over a new leaf," I said, getting up. "Anyway, what's up?"

"I've got some news. Guess who showed up at the clubhouse?"

"I don't know. Who?"

"Cole Davis."

That woke me up. "What did he want?"

"He said he had some intel to give us on the Devil's Rangers."

"Now, why in the fuck would he do that?"

"Because he's pissed off that they set up his sister for the death of Slammer. Guess he spoke to Raina earlier this morning. She told him how we helped rescue her son and now he wants to help us in any way he can."

It sounded legit, but I didn't know Cole. I knew the Devil's Rangers, however, and those guys would do anything to take us down. This could be a set-up. "What's your take on the guy?"

"Honestly, I think he's telling the truth. When I met him, he looked like he'd been in a fight."

"Huh. What kind of information did he give you?"

"Said that his V.P., Ronnie Jenkins, was the one who told him that we were responsible for the drive-by that almost killed Billy. He learned from another source that Ronnie had no idea who was really responsible, but decided to use it to their club's advantage. So he blamed us, which started a domino-effect. Apparently, when Cole confronted the V.P. about it last night, they got into a fist-fight."

"Did Ronnie admit to anything?"

"Not in so many words, but check this out – Cole said that Ronnie was related to Reaper. They were cousins."

"No shit? I guess that shouldn't surprise anyone."

"So, what do you think we should do?"

"I don't know. Let's hold a meeting later this afternoon, and we'll discuss it."

"Sounds good. What do you want to do about Cole?"

"He still at the clubhouse?"

"Yeah. He believes Ronnie has put a 'hit' out on him."

"Why?"

"He told him he was going to us with the information and that's when things got physical."

"Sounds like Cole is fucked unless we help him."

"Probably. He's worried about his sister, too."

My eye twitched. "Did they threaten her?"

"He was given the impression that both of their lives were in danger."

"Jesus," I said, closing my eyes. I rubbed my forehead. "Looks like we've got some more shit to clean up."

"Yeah. We owe the bastards anyway."

"What did Cole say about his role in killing Slammer?" I asked, curious.

"Said he drove Raina and even told her it was a bad idea. She wasn't in her right mind, he admitted."

"Her killing him wasn't personal," I said. "We've talked about it and she feels like shit about the entire deal. Was even going to turn herself in for his murder."

"Maybe she should."

"She's got a son to take care of and her going to prison isn't going to solve anything."

"It sounds like you're not blaming her."

"Just like I said before, I blame the Devil's Rangers. They set him up and she killed my old man because she thought he was responsible for Billy's death. I think we'd all do the same, especially in that state of mind."

He sighed. "Yeah."

"Okay, I'll be back in town by three. Let everyone know we're holding church at four."

"You're not in Jensen? Where the fuck you at?"

"I'm still in Waterloo."

"Why?"

"I decided to stay the night and enjoy the sights," I joked.

"You met a woman out there, didn't you?"

I didn't reply.

He laughed. "Yes, you did. Is she from the hospital? You've always wanted to bang a woman in white."

"I gotta go and take a piss."

"Fine. Keep it to yourself. You'll spill the beans later. You just can't help yourself."

"Don't hold your breath waiting," I said, smiling.

"Whatever. I'll see you when you get here."

"Tell Cole to stick around. If he's telling us the truth, we'll offer him protection."

"If he's not telling us the truth?"

"You already know, brother."

"Yeah, I figured."

THIRTY EIGHT

RAINA

JUSTIN SHOWED UP at the door around eleven, with coffee and a large bag of food. I'd just gotten dressed and Joanna was using the bathroom.

"I thought you wanted to go somewhere and eat?" I said, letting him into the room. The food smelled delicious, however. So, I was glad we didn't have to wait.

"Sorry. No time for that," he replied, setting everything onto the dresser. "I have some things to take care of back in Jensen, so I brought breakfast to you." He turned to my son. "Billy, do you like pancakes?"

He stared up at him shyly. "Yes."

"I was hoping you'd say that. Here you go, bud," Justin said, holding up a plastic container. "There's syrup and butter inside, too."

"Fank you," Billy replied.

"Good manners. I like that," said Justin.

"Fanks," Billy said.

I grabbed the pancakes from Justin. "I'll take that. Thanks for doing this."

"You bet. I wasn't sure what you and Joanna wanted. I just picked up some egg and bacon breakfast croissants and a couple containers of fruit and yogurt."

"That sounds wonderful," I replied, my stomach growling.

Joanna walked out of the bathroom. "I thought I heard you out here," she said. "Oh, you brought food and coffee. I could just kiss you! In fact, I will."

"I figured you might want something to get you going for the ride ahead," he said, looking at me as Joanna leaned over and kissed him on the cheek.

"Yes and this will hit the spot," she said, grabbing one of the hot Styrofoam cups.

"There are cream and sugar packets in the bag," he said. "There's also orange juice for Billy. I wasn't sure what to get him."

"You did great," I replied, grabbing the orange juice out of drink-carrier.

"What about you?" asked Joanna, grabbing a sandwich out of the bag.

"I already ate," he said.

"Oh. Okay," she replied.

"Have you heard anything new about..." his voice trailed off as he looked over at Billy. "You know."

"No," she replied. "All I know is that as of nine o'clock this morning, he's still missing."

"Do you have any other homes besides the two?" Justin asked her.

"No, and I have no idea where he might have taken off to. For all I know, he has a fake ID and is already on a plane heading to some tropical paradise. If we're lucky, it will crash."

Smirking, Justin took a sip of coffee. "Is there anyone else on his side of the family who might hide him?"

"From what I know, Betty was the last living relative," she replied. "Right, Raina?"

"Yes. At least from what we know."

"I'm sure they'll find him, eventually. If not, my club knows of someone that's really good at tracking people."

"Who's that? A bounty hunter?"

He smiled. "Basically. He hasn't failed us yet in finding someone."

"Is he expensive?" I asked.

"Who cares," said Joanna, quickly. "To be honest, I'm a little frightened of going home and sleeping in my house. I can only stay with my mother for so long, you know?"

"Why you scaywed?" asked Billy.

"I'm not, honey," she said, now regretting the comment.

He looked confused. "But, you said…"

"Aunt Joanna has nothing to be scared about," I said. "She was just joking around."

"Yes," Joanna said. "In fact… the only person around here that should be scared is you… if you don't eat those delicious looking pancakes. I'm going to steal them from you if they don't disappear soon."

Billy giggled. "Leave dem alone."

"What if I don't leave you alone?" She reached over and tickled his tummy.

He burst out laughing. "Stop!"

Their banter continued as I grabbed a yogurt cup out of the bag. Just listening to the sound of Billy laughing was enough to put a smile on my face.

Justin moved closer to me. "Can I talk to you alone?" he murmured.

"Sure," I said, setting the yogurt onto the dresser.

"We'll be right back," said Justin, grabbing my hand.

Joanna looked at us curiously. "Where you going?"

He nodded toward Billy. "I have some stuff to talk to her about that doesn't involve little ears."

"Gotcha," she replied, her eyes twinkling. "I'd keep it down, though. You two were talking pretty loudly last night."

I stared at her in surprise.

She grinned. "These walls are much thinner than they should be."

Blushing, I turned to Billy, who was thankfully clueless to our conversation. "I'll be right back, honey."

"Okay," he said, chewing on a pancake.

We left the room and went back to Justin's.

"What's up?" I asked, when he closed the door behind us.

Justin pulled me into his arms and kissed me deeply. When he was finished, he stared down at me. "Damn, woman. Even kissing you gets me hard."

Feeling horny myself, I touched his zipper, which was bulging. "You're not lying."

"If you're going to touch me there, you're going to have to face the consequences," he said, pulling me over to the bed.

I stopped abruptly. "Number one – there's no time. Number two – I thought I told you this couldn't happen again."

"You said you'd think about it," he replied.

"I haven't had time to think. I slept like a rock and have only been up long enough to have a shower."

Justin pulled me to him again. "Did you think about me when you were in there?" he asked, nuzzling my neck. "When your body was all wet and sudsy."

Closing my eyes, I felt my womanhood tingle. "Maybe."

"Come on now. Be honest. Did you touch yourself?" he whispered, nibbling on my earlobe.

242

"Yes," I admitted.

He groaned. "I'm not letting you out of here until I get another taste of that sweet pussy of yours," he said, pulling my dress up and over my hips. "Fuck me, you're not wearing panties." He ran his finger along my slit, which was already wet.

"Oh, God. Justin," I breathed, as he slid a finger inside of my slick hole.

"You still sore?" he asked huskily, moving it around.

"I... don't... know," I said and then moaned.

Grabbing the television remote with his other hand, he turned on the television. "Darlin, I'm not letting you out of here until we find out," he said, turning up the volume.

I knew that I should protest, but I couldn't find the words. Especially when he got to his knees, grabbed my hips, and pulled my lower lips to his. Sliding his tongue between my slit, he worked me until I was gasping in pleasure and grinding against his face.

"That's it, come for me," he growled against my crotch.

Staring down at the sexy man burying his face between my legs sent me over the edge. This time I clamped my mouth shut, emitting a high-pitched squeak instead of last night's wail of delight.

Justin chuckled and stood up. "What in the hell was that?"

I giggled. "I don't know."

He unbuttoned his jeans. "This time, I want to hear you scream my name," he said, pushing me over to the bed. "Get on your knees."

Aching to feel him inside of me, I did what he asked and looked over my shoulder.

"That's it," he said, coming up behind me, completely naked

now with his angry, red cock bobbing up and down. "You ready for me, darlin'?"

"Yes," I said, spreading my legs wider. Sore or not, I couldn't wait for him to fill me up.

"I don't think you are." He leaned down and licked my opening again.

"Yes, I am. Please, just do it already," I begged.

He ran his hands over my ass and squeezed. "I thought you didn't want me to fuck you anymore."

I laughed coldly. "Don't even go there right now."

"You sure you want it?" he asked, shoving a finger into my hole. He added a second one.

"Yes," I said, pushing against his hand.

"Tell me you want it."

"I want it."

"Tell me you want *me*."

"Yes. I want you, Justin," I moaned as he fucked me with his two fingers.

He rubbed my clit with the other hand. "You still need to think about it some more?"

"No," I whimpered, feeling another orgasm begin to build.

Breathing hard himself, he pulled his fingers out and pressed the tip of his cock against my opening. Grabbing my hips, he plunged inside of me.

"You are so fucking tight," he said, clenching his teeth. He pulled out slightly and then thrust into me again. "Does this hurt?"

"Yes, but... it's so good."

"That's all I needed to hear," he said, going faster.

I closed my eyes and gasped with each movement of his hips, his mammoth cock filling and stretching me. A tingling from somewhere deep inside began to grow as he angled his penis, hitting what I could only decipher as being my G-spot. He leaned over me and began rubbing my clit.

"That feel good, too?"

"Yes," I moaned

"You want me to stop?"

"No."

"You don't need to think about it for a while?"

Knowing that he was going to keep torturing me for what I'd said, earlier, I told *him* to stop.

He stiffened up. "What?"

I crawled out from under Justin and then turned to face him. "Lie down," I ordered, snapping my fingers.

He gave me a funny smile and then got on his back.

I crawled on top of him and slid down onto his cock slowly. "So... you like to be in charge?" I asked, moving my hips in a circular motion.

"Most of the time," he said, staring up at me with red-hot lust.

Not taking my eyes off of him, I pulled my dress off and flung it to the floor. Then I removed my bra slowly.

Licking his lips, he grabbed my breasts and squeezed.

I slapped his hands away. "No."

"No?" he pouted.

"I'm in charge this time," I said, smiling down at him wickedly.

I ran my hands over his muscular chest. "Whether you like it or not."

"I… like it."

"Good." I moved my hips slowly, taking pleasure in the way he was staring up at me. Like I owned him. Right now, I knew that I did. "Do you want me to go faster, Mr. President?"

He grinned. "Fuck yes."

"You do huh? Tell me – how does it feel to want, Tank?" I teased, leaning over him so that my breasts hung inches from his face. "That's what they call you, right?"

"Yes and it makes me want to come all over your tits. That's what it makes me want," he said, reaching for them again.

I sat up and knocked his palms away again. "No touching unless I allow you to." I shook them playfully.

"You are an evil bitch, you know that?" he said, smiling coldly.

I clenched my kegel muscles.

Justin sucked in a breath and then chuckled.

"You're lucky we don't have a lot of time or I'd show you just how evil I can be. Now, I want *you* to fuck me like you mean it. If you think you can handle it."

"Darlin', let's see if you can handle *me.*" Justin grabbed the side of my hips and began fucking me hard, our movements shaking the bed so much, I thought it was going to collapse.

"Yes," I gasped, rubbing my clit. The sensation of him plunging into me while I masturbated was indescribable.

Watching, he reached up and captured one of my breasts. "That turns me on like fuck. Rub that pussy."

I stared down at him, moaning as my fingers moved. Everything about him excited me. From those penetrating green eyes, to his muscles and tats.

Clenching his jaw, he grabbed both my hips again. "I'm going to come."

I threw my head back as my own orgasm began to unfold. Grabbing his hand, I placed it over my mouth to stifle my cries as it shuddered through me. "Justin…."

Feeling my pelvic muscles contract, he gasped and then stiffened up, joining me in my climax. When we were both spent, he pulled my face down to his and kissed me with so much passion, it took my breath away.

"That was amazing," he said against my mouth. "I don't think I've ever come so hard in my life."

"It *was* amazing," I said, pulling away slowly. I smiled down at him and got up.

He ran his hand through his hair. "Damn, I hope Billy didn't hear any of that."

"The television is pretty loud. I doubt it."

He got up and walked into the bathroom.

I grabbed my dress. "So, that's why you brought me here? For sex?"

"Actually, no," he said, walking back out. He started getting dressed, too. "I wanted to talk to you about your brother."

"What about him," I asked.

"You spoke to him earlier today, right?"

"As a matter of fact, I did. How did you know?"

"I guess he didn't tell you what he did?"

"What *did* he do?" I asked, worried.

He told me about Cole showing up at their clubhouse.

"I knew he was going to leave the other club, but I knew nothing about the fight. Is he okay?" I asked.

"Yes. He's under my protection right now. So are you."

"What do you mean?" I asked, frowning.

"Cole thinks that your and Billy's lives are at risk."

"You've got to be kidding? The Devil's Rangers are now after *us*?"

"Apparently."

I put my hand to my forehead and closed my eyes. I just couldn't catch a break. "This is ridiculous. I didn't do anything to them."

"Just your association with your brother has put you in danger. But, don't worry, princess. I won't let them hurt you or your son."

I opened my eyes and began to pace. "Seriously, I don't have time for this. I need to get Billy back to school and see what I'm going to do about running Sal's, if he still wants me to." I bit the side of my lip. "You know, maybe I can stay at the bar for a while. There's a vacant apartment upstairs."

"Hold up, now. You're not going to be staying anywhere but with me."

I turned around and looked at him. "What?"

"I can't protect you unless you're close, so... you're going to stay at the clubhouse until we get this shit settled."

The clubhouse?!

No way.

"I can't do that!" I said shrilly.

He grabbed my shoulders. "First of all, settle the fuck down. You're only going to scare your son in the next room, okay?"

I took a deep breath and released it slowly. "Okay. I'll calm down but, seriously, I can't stay there. I *won't* stay there."

"You have to, Raina. They're after you and Cole. Besides, do you really want to risk Billy's life?"

"No," I said, my eyes filling with tears. I'd just gotten my son back and the thought of him being in danger, yet again, made me want to go on a killing spree. I'd take out every fucking Devil's Ranger that threatened his life if I had to.

"So, then think this through. Sensibly. You're staying at the clubhouse until we know your life is no longer in danger. You feel me?"

I rubbed my forehead. "There's no other way?"

"No."

Something told me that he was pleased there was no better choice. Now he could keep me within reach. "What about Cole?"

He shrugged. "He'll stay with us, too. If he wants."

I felt nauseated by the idea of living in a biker clubhouse. I'd heard the stories of what went on in those places. "Can't we just go to the cops and see if there's something that they can do?"

"They won't do anything unless you've already been attacked."

I knew he was right. They weren't even able to help us track down Billy's killers. "Okay," I replied, not having any other choice. "I guess we have to."

He relaxed. "It's a wise choice. I'm glad you're being cautious about this. You already know what these guys are capable of."

"Yeah. Unfortunately, I do."

When I'd spoke to Cole earlier, he'd told me how he'd discovered that Ronnie had lied about Slammer being responsible for the drive-by. He'd been disgusted by the idea and told me he was walking away from the Devil's Rangers. I guess Sal had been right, you can't just walk away from a club like that.

Justin grabbed my hand and brought it to his lips. "You have my word that I will do everything in my power, to keep you and your son safe."

Staring up into his eyes, I could tell he meant every word. I only hoped he was able to pull it off.

THIRTY NINE

RAINA

WHEN WE WALKED back to the other room, Joanna and Billy were gone and there was a woman changing the sheets.

"Oh. Hello there." She reached into her pocket and pulled out a slip of paper. "This is probably for you," she said, handing me a note. It said that Billy and Joanna were waiting for us, down in the lobby.

I looked at the clock; it was just after twelve, which I realized was the hotel's check-out time.

"Oops," said Justin, smirking. "Looks like we're breaking rules together already."

"You're a bad influence," I joked.

"I guess so. But you seemed to enjoy being bad a little while ago."

I grinned. "I plead the fifth."

"Did they leave anything behind?" he asked, scanning the room.

"I'm not sure."

"Take a look around, just in case."

I stepped into the bathroom, where I'd left my purse. Not finding it, I imagined that Joanna had taken it with her, along with my cell phone.

"I don't see anything," called Justin.

I walked out of the bathroom. "Me neither. I think we're good to go. Thank you," I told the cleaning lady.

She smiled. "You're welcome."

We went down to the lobby and looked around. There was no sign of them.

"Maybe they went in there," Justin said, pointing toward the swimming pool area.

"Billy loves swimming pools," I said, turning in that direction. We spent the next several minutes searching the atrium and then the entire ground floor of the hotel. When we still couldn't find either of them, I began to panic.

"Stay calm. It's a big hotel. We might have just missed them. Do you have your phone?" Justin asked.

"No. I would have called her by now," I said a little too sharply. He frowned.

I let out a sigh. "Sorry. I'm just worried."

"It's going to be fine. I'm going to go and check the parking lot. You go and talk with Guest Services. See if they remember the two of them checking out."

"Okay."

We split up and I went over to the front desk, where we'd checked in. When I asked the attendant about Joanna and Billy, the woman smiled.

"Yes, they checked out just a little while ago."

"Did you see them leave the hotel?"

"No, we were busy with other patrons and I didn't notice," she said and apologized. "Do you have the woman's phone number?"

"It's in my cell phone, but I couldn't tell you what it was," I said, frustrated. I turned toward the front and saw Justin heading back inside. From the look on his face, the news wasn't good. "You didn't find them, did you?"

"No," he said, running a hand over his face, "and the car is gone."

"What?" I walked around him and went outside. Now I wasn't

just worried, I was angry.

Where in the hell had she taken my son?

My eyes scanned the parking lot. The car definitely wasn't in its spot.

"Did you need some help, ma'am?" asked a young valet, coming up behind me.

I turned to him. "I'm looking for a woman and a young boy who left here within the last half hour. Have you seen them?"

"Does he have a stuffed dog?"

"Yes," I said, relaxing a little. "You saw them?"

"They got into a silver car and left, about ten minutes ago."

"Were they alone?" asked Justin, now joining us.

"Actually, there was a man with them. Tall and thin, with glasses. The little boy was holding his hand and looked excited to see him."

"Oh, my God," I said, feeling faint. I turned to Justin. "It has to be Phillip."

FORTY

TANK

RAINA LOOKED VERY pale and like she was about to pass out. "Come on," I said, grabbing her hand. I pulled her toward my motorcycle. "Do you have any idea where they might have gone?"

"No," she replied. "Oh, my God, he has my son again. What are we going to do?"

"Call the police," I said. My guys weren't around and I knew we needed to take action right away. I pulled my phone out and dialed nine-one-one. When they picked up, I explained the situation.

"What's the license plate number?" I asked Raina.

She gave it to me and I repeated it to the operator.

"We'll send out an A.P.B. right away," promised the woman.

"Thanks."

After I hung up, I placed another call.

"Raptor, I need your help." I explained what was happening and asked if he could contact the Judge.

"I'll try, but I think he's out of town on business."

"Just see if you can have him call me, brother," I said, placing my hand on Raina's shoulder. "Something tells me we're going to need his help. Especially if the police can't find them."

"I'll give him a call," he promised.

I hung up and pulled Raina into my arms. "We'll find them, darlin'. I swear to God, we will."

ANCHORAGE, ALASKA

FORTY ONE

JUDGE

I'D JUST STARTED packing up the stuff in my shed, when I received a call from Raptor.

"What's up?" I asked, putting down the packing-tape.

"We need your help," he said.

I groaned inwardly. "You know I've got my own shit to deal with right now." Like getting my life in order so that I could get my ass back to Jessica. It had only been a couple of days since I'd last seen her, and I was already missing her like crazy.

Raptor sighed. "I know. I know. I wouldn't ask you to help if it didn't involve a missing child."

I stiffened up. "It's not Sammy, is it?"

"No."

Raptor spent the next several minutes filling me in on the details.

"Whoa... wait a second. You mentioned a woman named Raina. Is she the person who killed Slammer?" I asked, recalling the last conversation I had with the guy.

"Yes."

I closed my eyes. "Fuck. He told me about her. Goddamn it."

"Slammer did? What did he say?"

"That she was looking for him. That she blamed him for killing her son. Now you're saying her son is *alive*?"

He told me about her brother-in-law and then went over the story of how, using some kind of drug, were able to make the boy appear dead.

"Sounds like a Lifetime movie," I said, still pissed off at myself. Had I intervened, somehow, Slammer might still be alive.

"I can't believe he didn't say anything to the rest of us. When did he talk to you about it?"

"When that thing with Jessica was going on. He said he could handle it, though. Why in the hell are you guys helping her now?"

"Tank's sweet on the woman."

"You're kidding me?"

"No. He thinks she's a victim, too. To be honest, I think he's falling for her."

I sighed. Tank was too soft-hearted. It was going to be his undoing. "Frankly, she is a victim," I said, matter-of-factly. "But I'm a little surprised that he's able to push aside what happened, especially to that extent." Falling for his father's killer didn't sound rational. Of course, I wasn't one to judge.

"I know. Me, too. Anyway, this isn't about her. It's about an innocent child and that's why something needs to be done."

"Fine. What do you need from me?"

"Any information that you can get for us, especially addresses."

"Hold on. I need to get into my cabin so I can write this down," I said, walking out of the shed.

"You have a cabin?" he asked.

I hadn't told him much about my personal life, more for his safety than anything.

"Yeah."

"Must be rough."

I actually owned two cabins, side-by-side. The one I was staying at was listed under the ownership of an Annabelle Gertrude Hunter. The one next door was supposed to have been given to Sammy, someday. Unfortunately, now, it was nothing but a crime-scene and the police were still trying to contact the property owner. This person wasn't an easy cat to locate.

"It has its moments," I said, stepping into the kitchen. I grabbed a piece of paper and a pen. "So, what do you have for me?"

"Names. First off – Phillip Davis. He's the man we think has the child. His wife is Joanna Davis. They live in Davenport, I believe she said. He's a surgeon at St. Luke's and she's an attorney."

"Didn't you say that Joanna was helping Raina?"

"Yes. I'm pretty sure she's being held against her will. Although, who knows. She might be part of it."

"Okay. What about that doctor you were telling me about. The scientist?"

"Jacob Slether. He's being held by the police right now. They're trying to charge him with kidnapping and murder."

"Will it stick?"

"There's a pretty solid case against him."

I wrote the name down anyway. "Okay. I'll make some phone calls and see if I can come up with any other addresses or intel on the Davis couple that might help us."

"Appreciate it," said Raptor. "Meanwhile, I'll keep you informed, too."

"Sounds good."

We hung up and I made a few phone calls to some friends with connections. After I was finished, I went into my bedroom and called Jessica.

"When are you coming back?" she asked breathlessly.

I lay down on the bed and stared up at the ceiling fan. "I've got some more things to take care of, here in Alaska. Then I need to go to Vegas."

"Vegas?"

"Yeah. For a new ID."

"That's right." She sighed. "I miss you."

"I miss you, too," I said, closing my eyes. I pictured her face, her lips, and her soft curves. Iowa seemed like it was on the other side of the world.

"Can I come to Vegas with you?"

I sat up. Admittedly, the thought of her joining me in Vegas was intriguing. "Do you have time? What about your job in Minnesota?"

"Actually, I'm not starting until the end of September now."

I smiled. "How'd you pull that off?" I asked. The last I'd heard, she was only a couple of weeks away from her residency.

"I told them about my stepfather's death and they gave me more time. So, what do you say? Vegas. You and me?"

"Okay."

"Okay?" she repeated, a smile in her voice.

"Yeah."

"Oh, my God," she squealed. "When?"

"Next Friday?"

"I can't believe it," she said. "I thought I wouldn't be seeing you until next month and now we're going to Vegas together."

"Obviously you've got to keep this quiet."

"Of course. I can tell my mother though, can't I?"

As much as I didn't want her to, I knew that Frannie would

panic if she didn't know where her daughter was or with whom. "Yes, but make sure she keeps this information to herself."

"What about Tank?"

I frowned. "Yeah, he should probably know, too. And Raptor. But that's it. Nobody else."

"I understand."

I saw a car pull up to the cabin.

Who the fuck is this now?

"Darlin', I've gotta go. I'll call you back later."

"Okay," she said, sounding disappointed.

"I love you, Jessica," I said, peering outside. Recognizing the car and the woman getting out of it, I groaned inwardly.

"I love you, too, Jordan."

We finished our goodbyes and I hung up the phone.

The doorbell rang.

Grabbing my gun, I shoved it into the waistband of my jeans and went to answer the door.

"Hello, stranger," said Caitlyn Ferraro, who, as always, was dressed to kill. Tonight, she had on a pale silk blouse and a short black skirt that showed off her legs. They were nice, but the only legs on my mind were Jessica's.

"I'm sorry, have we met?" I asked, giving her my best poker-face.

She chuckled. "You are so full of shit. Can I come in?"

"No."

Ignoring me, she pushed herself inside of the cabin and looked around. "Well this is rather quaint. I'd have expected something much better."

"Is that right?"

"Yes. I guess in your position, there's no time for extravagance."

"What do you want?" I asked, rubbing the back of my neck. There was no use pretending with her.

"You stood me up. We were supposed to continue our little chat."

"That was weeks ago and I'm sorry, but shit happened and I had to leave town."

She turned around and looked at me. "Yeah, I heard that there was a big shoot-out up in this area. Gang related."

"That's what I heard, too."

Caitlyn walked over to me and touched my shoulder.

I flinched.

She threw her head back and laughed. "Oh, my God. Are you actually afraid of me?"

You're a crazy broad, I wanted to say. *Hell, yeah I'm afraid of you.*

I snorted. "No. Of course not."

She began undressing me with her eyes and I knew I had to get her out of my cabin before she stripped down to nothing and tried whipping me with something again.

"Relax," she said, noticing my expression. "I'm not here for that. As much as I'd love to fuck you, I'm not going to beg for it. Not anymore."

I relaxed slightly. "So, what are you here for?"

"I need money."

I stared at her in disbelief. "Money?"

She nodded. "I owe someone some money and if I don't pay them... I'm afraid of what might happen."

"I don't know how I'm supposed to help you with that."

"You owe me."

"How do you figure?"

"The information I gave you. I'm pretty sure if I wouldn't have done it, your precious little Jessica wouldn't be alive today."

"I already knew she was being hunted, sweetheart."

"Well, I could have turned you in to the authorities. I still can," she said, smiling.

"You're threatening me?"

Her face seemed to crumble before my eyes. "I have no other choice. These guys will kill me if I don't pay them the money."

I stared at her hard. "How much do you owe them and why?"

"One-hundred-grand."

My eyes widened. "Why?"

Her lips began to tremble. "I'd rather not say."

"Why, Caitlyn?" I repeated. "You can't spring this on me and then clam up."

"Fine. I had them kill someone."

"Who?"

"My stepfather."

"Why?"

It took her awhile, but she eventually admitted that he'd molested her, growing up, and now he'd started in on another girl.

"He remarried, about five years ago, after my mother died. His new stepdaughter is only fifteen and he... he's doing the same thing to her."

"Why didn't you go to the police instead of having him killed?"

"Because she wouldn't admit it to me. But, I knew," said Caitlyn, openly crying now. "I could tell. I just wanted to help her."

"Did you try talking to your mother?"

"Yes, but she didn't believe it. She even threw me out of the house, saying that I was trying to cause trouble." She started sobbing. "I couldn't let him do the things that he did to me... to her. I couldn't."

Sighing, I pulled her into my arms. "It's okay."

"I'm sorry. I just didn't know where to turn. These men... they said they'd do it for twenty-grand. That was the agreement."

"They killed him for twenty?"

"Yes and now they're threatening to kill *me* if I don't come up with one-hundred."

"Who are they?" I asked, pulling away from her. She was getting too comfortable in my arms.

"Just these two dimwits that I met."

"Where did you meet them?"

She explained that she'd met the two guys at a bar, late one night. Both went home with her and eventually, they had a threesome. This occurred a few more times and eventually she started opening up to them. One night, she told them about her stepfather after drinking far too much, and it was then that they offered to kill him.

"And now they're blackmailing you?"

"Yes."

"Look, I'm not going to give you money. They don't deserve it."

"You're not going to help me?"

"I never said that."

Her eyes widened. "What are you going to do?"

266

"Make sure they don't bother you again."

"How?"

"It's better that you don't know."

She looked like a giant weight had been taken off of her shoulders. "You'll really do it? Help me?"

"Yes. Just give me their names and anything else you can tell me about them."

"I guess, the two bastards deserve whatever is coming to them." She opened up her purse and pulled out a piece of paper. "Here are their names," she said, writing them down. "I don't know where they live, but hopefully you can figure that part of it out."

"What bar do they usually hang out at?" I asked "Write that down too."

"Okay."

"If I do this, I need something from you."

"What?" she asked, now sounding hesitant.

"A plane," I said. As soon as I got rid of the two pricks, I wanted to get the hell out of Alaska without waiting around for a commercial flight.

"Barney's?"

I nodded. "Yes. I just need to borrow it for a couple of weeks. I'll get it back to you."

She bit her lower lip. "I don't know. My husband might find out that it's gone and report it stolen."

"Tell him you're renting it out to a friend."

"Yeah, I can do that. He doesn't fly himself, so it probably won't get missed anyway. Not until he plans on selling it, that is.

Regardless, I'll make it happen."

I leaned over and kissed her forehead. "You're a beautiful woman. Quit giving yourself away."

"My husband won't touch me anymore," she said with a sad smile.

"Then get yourself a new husband. Not a bunch of one-night stands who might try blackmailing you again," I said, walking into the bathroom. I grabbed a box of tissues and brought it back out to her. "Here."

She took one and wiped her eyes. "No matter what I've heard about you, I know the truth. You're a good man, Jordan."

That wasn't really true, but I was working on it…

FORTY TWO

RAINA

JUSTIN TRIED HIS best to calm me down, but I felt like I was losing my mind.

"We have to go look for them. Let's go back to the cabin and see if they took Billy there."

"It's a crime scene right now. He wouldn't risk taking them back there."

"Then what do we do?"

"We wait for the police to do their job," he said.

I groaned. "Yeah, right. I think we should try looking for them ourselves."

"I'm all for that. What do you suggest?" he replied, folding his arms across his chest.

"I don't know. Let's just start driving through town. It's better than waiting around here," I said, feeling helpless.

"I agree."

"I don't' know what I'm going to do if I don't find my son," I said hoarsely.

"We'll find him." He grabbed my hand and led me to his Harley, a black Road King. Justin got on first and then handed me his helmet. We drove to the cabin and when we arrived, both of us were surprised to see that the place was dead.

"Where is everyone?" I asked, expecting to see cops still wandering around the property.

Justin shut off the bike. "There was only one murder and it was pretty cut-and-dried. They have their witnesses and probably have all of the other evidence that they need by now."

"Still, I'm surprised," I replied, getting off of his motorcycle.

"Maybe they did come back this way," he said, staring toward the lake. He removed his sunglasses and his eyes widened. "Holy shit. Watch out."

The next thing I know, Justin was off of the bike and flying toward the water. When I noticed the eighteen-foot Stingray boat being untied at the dock, my heart almost gave out.

It was Phillip and Billy.

Phillip had his back to us; he didn't even notice Justin racing toward them. At least, not until Billy turned around and pointed it out.

"Billy!" I screamed, running toward the lake.

Meanwhile, Justin successfully made it to the edge of the dock and leaped onto the boat before Phillip could start the engine. He landed on his back and I watched as both men went down.

"Mommy!" cried Billy, looking frightened as fists began to fly.

The untied boat began drifting toward the weeds.

"Help, mommy!"

"Hold on!" I hollered, diving into the water. Ignoring the pain in my thigh, I swam over and climbed on board.

"Enough," shouted Phillip, who was now holding a gun toward Justin. I recognized it as being the one I'd been hiding in my purse. The one that had killed Slammer.

Dammit, I should have gotten rid of it, I thought. *Cole had been right.*

"Phillip, what are you doing?" I asked, trembling now.

He glared at me. "Don't either of you move, or I'll blow your damn heads off."

Justin raised his hands in the air. "Settle down," he said. "It doesn't have to be like this."

Phillip aimed the gun at me. "This is all your fault, you stupid bitch. You just had to put your nose where it didn't belong."

"Where it didn't belong?" I repeated angrily. "This is my son. You stole him from me!"

"You're not fit to be a mother to this boy. Look at the kind of people you hang out with!?" he spat, waving his gun toward Justin. "Scumbags like this."

"Mommy, I'm scawed," sobbed Billy as I held him against my chest.

"See. You're scaring him," I said, trying not to cry. "Put the gun down, Phillip."

Phillip's eyes softened. "Billy, come here," he said, ignoring me. "You know I'd never hurt you. Come to daddy."

"You are *not* his daddy," I said, clenching my teeth.

"Shut up," said Phillip. "Now, Billy, come here."

Billy shook his head.

Phillip's eye twitched. "Remember what we talked about, son?"

Shaking his head, he clung to me even tighter.

"Put the gun down," said Justin. "Before someone gets hurt."

Phillip cocked the gun. "I'm going to count to ten. If you're not off of this boat, I'm going to start shooting and yes, someone will get hurt."

"No," I said, raising my hand. "Don't do it. Please."

He began to count.

"This is insane. You're not a killer!" I cried, knowing that we were losing control of the situation. "You're Billy's uncle. He adores you! Phillip, this isn't how you want him to remember you."

He laughed harshly. "Remember *me*? I'm not going anywhere. You're the one who's leaving this world. And this guy, too. Biker scumbag. It will be a better place without either of you. Believe me."

I pushed Billy behind me. "Just let us go. We won't even tell the police that you were here. Please."

The sound of a boat whizzing by drew Phillip's attention long enough for Justin to get to his ankle holster. He pulled out a gun and aimed it at Phillip. "Put your gun down," he hollered, cocking his own. "Now!"

Phillip's eyes narrowed.

"I mean it. Put the gun down or I'll shoot you right in the head."

"I see this isn't going to work out the way I planned," he said, looking irritated. "I guess if I'm not going to leave here with Billy, I don't want you to either."

"Don't. Please," I said, catching his meaning.

"Phillip pointed the gun at me. "I have to. You're not worthy enough to raise a Davis."

Justin snorted. "Really, dude? A Davis? *You're not worthy enough to raise a Davis*," he mimicked. "Tell me something – what's so fucking special about a 'Davis'?"

Phillip stared at him haughtily. "You're not one of them. That's what's so special."

Justin rolled his eyes and shot him in the head.

I FOUND JOANNA tied up in the cabin. When she saw me, she cried in relief. "Thank God! Have you seen Billy?"

"He's fine," I said, cutting the duct tape from her wrists with scissors.

"I'm so sorry," she cried. "He found us outside the hotel. He figured it out from the credit card I'd used to reserve the hotel room. I'm so stupid. I should have known better."

"It's okay. You're safe and so is Billy," I replied, giving her a reassuring hug.

"Where's Phillip?"

"He… he got away," I said, hiding the truth. I didn't want Justin arrested for killing the asshole. I'd been surprised that he'd pulled the trigger so quickly, but I knew if he wouldn't have, things would have only gotten uglier.

"Damn," she replied, rubbing her wrists. "Where are Billy and Justin?"

"Billy is on the deck. Justin took the boat out to try and find Phillip." He was actually taking Phillip's body to a desolate place, to hide it.

"We should call the police," she said.

"Already did," I said, forcing a smile. "They're trying to find him, too."

She sighed. "Good."

"Where's my car?" I asked.

"It's parked out in back."

"That's good. Do you have my purse and cell phone?"

"They're in the car, too. So are your keys. Phillip has the gun, though."

"Oh. Okay."

She let out a ragged sigh. "Are we free to leave now? I just want to get the hell out of this town."

"Same here."

"I'm having the locks changed as soon as we get home and buying a dog. A big mean one."

We walked outside, where Billy was seated. He was staring off toward the lake, a thoughtful expression on his face.

"Honey, are you okay?" I asked, bending down. I stared into his eyes. He'd heard the gun go off and knew that Phillip was dead. I'd made him promise not to tell anyone so Justin didn't go to jail. I knew it was a lot of weight to put on a young child and was worried about what that would do to him. "Billy?"

He nodded.

"He's been through so much," said Joanna, fluffing his hair.

"Yes. He's my brave little man."

Billy smiled at me.

"Are you ready to go home?" I asked him.

"Yes."

I held out my hand. "Me, too. Let's go get you into the car."

"Wait. We can't leave Tank."

My eyes softened. I thought it was cute how Billy was so worried about Justin. "We won't. Don't worry. You really like him, don't you?"

"Yes," he replied. "He's tough."

"Yes, he is," I answered. And not just physically. I wasn't sure what I'd have done without him. He was like a rock for us at the moment. I was glad that I'd accepted the offer to stay at his club.

TWO WEEKS LATER

FORTY THREE

RAINA

"W HAT'S THAT?" I asked, staring at the leather vest. "I told you before, I want you to be my old lady," Justin replied, holding the cut up proudly. "And this will let everyone else know to keep their hands off, because you belong to me."

I smirked. "I do, huh?"

He grabbed my butt. "I own this ass. You even said so last night."

"We were in the middle of having sex. I didn't mean it literally," I said, shooing his hand away. "Now, let me finish up, will you?"

We were in the room that Billy and I had been staying at in the clubhouse. We'd finally gotten the 'okay' to go home and I was just packing the rest of our things.

"You're telling me 'no'?" he pouted. "You won't wear my patch?"

I sighed. Not this again. "We've talked about all of this before. Billy and I don't belong in this… world," I said, waving my hand around the room. Admittedly, it hadn't been quite as bad as I'd thought.

"Come on now. It isn't as bad as you think and everyone loves you. They'd protect you and Billy with their lives."

I had gotten to know the members of his club and fortunately, after everything that had happened, they'd found it in their hearts to forgive me. Well, most of them. There were a couple guys who were still a little chaffed about Slammer and I couldn't blame them. Hell, three weeks ago, if anyone would have told me I'd be walking around the Gold Vipers clubhouse, that Cole would be a new Prospect, or that I'd be sharing a bed with Slammer's son, I'd have laughed in their face.

"If it was like this all the time, I'd be okay with it. But, some of the old ladies say that 'when it's good, it's really good. When it's bad, it's fire and brimstone'."

He let out a long sigh. "Forget about all of that. Forget about the club. How do you feel about us?"

"I like you. A lot," I replied, biting back a smile. The truth was, I loved him. I really did. I'd even told him once during sex, but it had come out a whisper.

"I think you secretly worship me," he said, pulling me into his arms.

I snored. "Right. Maybe your penis."

"That's what I thought. If you play nice, I'll let you bow down and kiss it. But, you have to let me see some boobies first."

"You goof. There's no time for this," I said, laughing as he tried pulling off my shirt. One thing I'd learned about him was that his mind was almost always on sex. Fortunately, he also had a great sense of humor. Admittedly, Justin was not at all what I'd expected out of biker club president. I'd have pictured an asshole, one who barked out orders and could cut you with a single look. The thing with him was that he almost always had a smile on his face and treated his brothers equally.

"All I need is thirty seconds," he said.

"We don't even have that. Did you forget that we have to finish up here and pick up Billy from Frannie's?"

His face became serious. "Oh shit. I forgot. Jessica's making dinner tonight. I told her we'd be there."

"But, you said that you'd help me move back to my apartment and...there's too much to do," I said, relieved that we were finally going home now that Ronnie was no longer a threat. Apparently, he'd disappeared and someone called the Judge had put the fear of God into the president of that chapter. Now, thankfully, the Devil's Rangers were no longer interested in me and I could bring my son home.

"You don't have to stay long. She's leaving for Vegas tomorrow and wants to make dinner for all of us. Including Raptor and Adriana."

"Sammy's going to be there, too?" Billy and Sammy had so much fun together.

"Yes. Billy won't want to leave if he finds out Sammy's coming over."

"True. Well, I owe it to her anyway. Both she and Frannie have been so good to Billy."

"They love him. Especially Frannie."

"The feeling is mutual," I said, thinking about the conversation that I'd had with Billy just the night before. He'd gone on and on about a trip to the zoo he'd had with Frannie. Now that I was spending more time at Sal's, learning about the business, I'd been dropping Billy off at her place in the evenings, and picking him up after my shift. He'd even spent a few nights there. "So, who is she going to Vegas with?"

"Raptor's brother. His name is Jordan Steele."

"Oh. I didn't know he had a brother," I said, stuffing more of Billy's clothes into a box.

"Yeah. Nor did he, until a couple of years ago. Anyway, to make a long story short – Jordan's been out of town for the last few weeks and he doesn't know it yet, but she's making this big dinner tonight. In honor of his return and their Vegas trip."

"Why not just make it for the two of them?"

He shrugged. "I'm not really sure. I think she's trying to get him around people more. He's kind of a hobbit."

I laughed and pictured a short guy with pointy ears and dirty feet. "A hobbit?"

"He doesn't like being around people much."

I snorted. "He sounds like quite the catch."

"She has the hots for him and he's good to her. That's all that matters."

"It could be something else," I replied, thinking about the dinner she had planned. "Maybe Jessica has an announcement to make. I mean, they *are* going to Vegas," I said, smiling. "Could be wedding bells in the near future."

His smile fell. "Wedding bells? They barely know each other."

I grinned and kissed his cheek. Justin was very protective of Jessica. "Honey, you and I hardly know each other."

"But, we're not getting married."

"You're asking me to wear your patch," I reminded him. "Isn't that almost the same thing?"

He shrugged.

"Just relax, big guy. Your sister knows what she's doing. I can see that she has her head screwed on right."

He grinned wickedly. "Speaking of 'head'."

I rolled my eyes.

FORTY FOUR

JESSICA

I STARED AT MYSELF in the mirror, wondering if I looked okay. It seemed like forever since I'd last seen Jordan and I was so nervous, I could barely put my mascara on. Leaning forward, I finished up my makeup and then wound my hair up into a messy bun. After inserting a few Bobby-pins to hold it in place, I went back to my bedroom, slipped off the robe, and put on the slinky black dress. I then headed downstairs to check on the prime rib I had baking in the oven. The entire house already smelled delicious and I couldn't wait for Jordan to try my first roast.

"What are you doing?" I asked my mother, who was also in the kitchen, apparently checking on things, too.

She turned around and looked at me innocently. "Nothing. Just making sure that everything is coming along nicely."

"You're in charge of the Caesar salad," I said, nodding toward the refrigerator. "And maybe the rolls." I also had a pot of potatoes and another with asparagus spears sitting on the stove, ready to boil. For dessert, I'd made a cherry cheesecake from scratch. This was a big night and I wanted everything perfect.

"That's fine. You look beautiful, by the way."

She also looked lovely in a silky, white blouse and beige slacks. Thankfully, she was finally getting her smile back, which I hadn't seen much of since Slammer's untimely death. "You do too, mother."

She smiled and gave me a hug. "So, when is the man of the hour showing up? I have yet to meet this mysterious stranger who's whisking my daughter to Vegas."

I looked at my watch. It was almost five. Dinner was at seven.

"I'm not sure. I suppose he could be showing up any time now."

"And he's not going to stand you up again?"

Unfortunately, he'd had to push out our trip to Vegas because of some things happening in Anchorage. His business there was finally finished, however, and now he would be mine for as long as I could keep him in my sights. "It wasn't by choice," I told her.

She sighed. "I just don't want him breaking your heart, honey. I mean, you really don't know Jordan all that well and now you're flying off to Vegas with the man."

My eyes narrowed. She was such an overprotective mother. She just didn't understand. "Besides you and Tank, he's the one person I trust with my life. If it wasn't for him, I might not even be here. That has to count for something, doesn't it?"

Frannie smiled. "Yes. I'm sorry. I'm just going to miss you."

"Billy will be around to keep you company," I said, thinking about Raina's son. My mother adored the little boy and I could tell she was hoping that Tank would patch Raina soon. I'd never seen my stepbrother so happy.

"It's not the same thing, and you know it," she said, looking into my eyes, hers sparkling. "You're not only my daughter, you're my best friend. Nobody could replace that."

I smiled. "I know and you're my best friend, too, mom. But, don't worry, we'll be back in no time. Then we can get ready to move out to Shoreview with Aunt Cheryl. Away from all of this biker business."

She crossed her arms under her chest. "About that. I know I said I'd think about it, but... I just don't think it's the right time for me to move."

My eyes widened. "But, you agreed that it was a great idea."

She nodded. "Yes, I know what I said. The thing is, my life is in Jensen and I'm not ready to uproot and leave right now."

I sighed.

"Then, there's Tank and little Billy. I told Raina that I was thinking about leaving the nursing home and offered to watch her son while she was at work."

Slammer's life-insurance policy had been for a substantial amount, and I knew my mother would never have to work again. "You did?" I asked, surprised.

She nodded. "Yes. The boy needs someone to care for him when his mother's away at work. Someone she can trust."

"What about the other club wives?"

"They have their own jobs and children to worry about. Sure, I know they'd help if she asked, but I'm available to do it and... I need someone to take care of. Now that Slammer is gone and you're leaving, this would be good for both him and me."

Seeing the love in my mother's eyes for Billy, I smiled. "He could definitely use a grandma," I said, knowing that Raina only had her brother, Cole and Uncle Sal, and no other living relatives. "Besides, if Tank marries her one day, you'll actually be his grandma."

She smiled. "That's what I'm hoping. He definitely loves her. I can tell."

"Me, too."

The doorbell rang, interrupting us.

"That's got to be him," I said, anxious and nervous at the same time.

"I'll get it," she said, turning to leave the kitchen.

"No, *I'll* get it. You'll scare him away," I teased, racing around her. I hurried to the door and opened it. Expecting Jordan, my face fell when I saw the older gentleman standing on our porch.

"Can I help you?" I asked, not recognizing the man with the white hair. He appeared to be in his sixties, wore thick eyeglasses, and had a moustache that curled up at the ends. He also had on a well-tailored dark suit and was holding a cane.

"Are you Jessica?" he asked, in a deep voice.

"Yes," I said, staring beyond him at the black limousine parked in front of our townhouse.

"Very good. I'm here to pick you up."

My head snapped back to him. "Pick *me* up?"

He smiled. "Yes. Jordan Steele is expecting you."

"There must be some mistake. He's supposed to come here," I replied, frowning.

"Sorry, miss. All I know is that he sent me to retrieve you."

"I'd better call him. No offense, the limo ride would be great, but I'm in the middle of cooking dinner. I can't just leave."

My mother joined us at the door. "What's going on?" she asked, looking confused.

"Jordan sent this limo for me."

Her face brightened. "Really?"

"I can't leave. I'm cooking a big dinner for everyone. There's still so much to do."

"Don't worry. I'll keep an eye on the food. Go ahead and see what this is all about."

"From what I hear, this won't take long and you'll be back in a jiffy," said the old man.

Excited to see Jordan, and wondering what this was all about, I gave in. "Okay. I guess I'd better do what he wants," I replied, walking back into the house. "Let me get my shoes."

"Very good, miss," said the driver.

I grabbed my new pair of black strappy heels, the ones I'd purchased specifically for that evening, and put them on.

"Do I need my purse?" I asked the man.

"I don't believe so."

"I should probably get my cell phone," I said, turning to go back inside.

"Actually, he said to bring you and not worry about those other things," said the man.

I thought it was a little strange, but I shrugged. "Okay. Let's go."

"This way, please. Oh, and ma'am, I'll have her back shortly," he told Frannie, stepping off of the porch.

"Take your time. Dinner isn't for another hour or so," she said, sounding amused.

"I'm sorry, what did you say your name was?" I asked, the driver.

"I didn't. You can call me Henry," he said with a friendly smile.

"Okay."

We walked to the limo and he opened the door for me. Looking inside, I was a little disappointed. I'd been hoping to find Jordan waiting for me.

"Everything okay?" he asked, noticing my glum expression.

"It's fine," I replied, getting into the vehicle. "Where are we going anyway?"

"It's a surprise," he said. "There's champagne in the bucket and a glass. Jordan said to tell you to start without him. He wants you to be comfortable."

"Okay," I said, crawling over to the champagne.

Henry shut the door and then got into the limo. The window between us was open and he turned his head. "There's music back there, too. Feel free to turn whatever you want on."

"Thanks," I said, popping the cork on the bubbly. I poured some into a glass and stuck the bottle back into the bucket of ice.

"All set?" asked the driver.

"Yes," I said, our eyes meeting in the mirror. It was then that I got a good look at his baby blues.

No way.

There was only one man who had eyes that color. He also loved to play games. "So," I said, biting back a smile as I took a sip of champagne. "You really can't tell me where we're going?"

"No," he replied, pulling away from the curb.

"I guess that shouldn't surprise me. Jordan is a mysterious guy."

"He is, huh?"

I took another sip of champagne. It warmed my stomach. "Yes. The man is amazing. I'm so excited to see him."

"I'm sure he feels the same way."

I drank a few more sips of the champagne and then set it down. Feeling wicked, I hiked my dress up a little higher. "You can't imagine what it's been like at night. Wanting him. It's been getting so bad that I've had to pleasure myself."

He coughed and our eyes met in the mirror again. I had to keep from laughing at his surprise.

"Pardon me?"

"I'm sorry. I don't know where that came from."

His eye twitched and he looked back at the road. "No problems, miss."

Enjoying myself, I leaned back on the seat and pulled my dress all the way up, exposing my red panties. "I'm sorry, but this champagne is going straight to my head."

Turning the corner, he didn't notice.

"I mean, just talking about it right now is making me hot," I said, sliding my fingers under the fabric. "You don't mind if I touch myself, do you?"

He looked back at me in the mirror, stunned.

"Can you hurry and find Jordan?" I said and then moaned. "I need him inside of me."

The limo jerked hard to the right and then came to a complete stop. I glanced outside and noticed that we were parked on the side of the road, near a residential neighborhood.

"Is he close?" I asked. "Because I... I certainly am."

He got out of the limo, slammed the door, and joined me in the back.

"Henry?" I said, feigning surprise. "What are you doing?"

"I'm going to spank the hell out of you," he said huskily.

I turned over and shook my rear. "Go ahead, Henry. You can spank me all you want... as long as you fuck me good, afterward, like Jordan."

"You little vixen." Jordan ripped off the glasses and then tore at the latex on his face. "How did you know?"

"I'd know those eyes anywhere," I said, turning back around. I reached for the wig and pulled it off. "Henry was a cute old man, but I want my sexy, young stud."

He grabbed my face and kissed me hard on the mouth. "I've missed you so much," he said, pulling my hair out of the bun. Bobby-pins flew everywhere as he ran his fingers through my waves.

"I've missed you, too," I said, grabbing at his neck tie. I tugged it off and began unbuttoning his shirt.

Jordan pushed me backward and then shoved my skirt up. Pulling my panties to the side, he buried his face between my legs, lapping at my womanhood.

I grabbed him by his hair and moaned as he added his fingers. It took only a few seconds to make me come. I screamed his name and begged him to fuck me.

And did he ever.

Within seconds, I had his pants down and was bouncing on his lap. The entire limo shook with each thrust of his hips.

Cupping my breasts, he licked and tugged at my nipples, sending delicious shivers directly to my sex.

"Yessssss..." I moaned, my womanhood spasming as I came a second time.

"Jessica," he gasped, his fingers gripping my hips tightly as he suddenly stopped moving. I could feel his penis pulsating inside of me as he came.

Holding him against me, I could smell the familiar scent of his cologne and closed my eyes, enjoying it.

"So, are you still upset that you had to leave the kitchen?" he asked, a smile in his voice.

I tipped his head back and looked into his eyes. "No. This beats cooking any day."

"I just had to have you to myself for a few minutes before dinner."

"I'm glad you did."

He pulled my face to his and kissed my lips. "I missed you."

"I missed you, too."

We clasped hands.

"I have something to tell you," I said, running my hand through his hair to fix his bangs. "It's kind of important."

"You're pregnant."

I laughed. "No."

"Thank God," he said, sighing in relief.

"Very funny. You'd make a great father. You know that don't you?"

"I don't know how to be a father," he said, his smile leaving.

"Nobody does when they start out, Jordan. You take one day at a time and hope for the best."

"You make it sound so easy."

"Everyone knows that children aren't easy. Something tells me that you can handle it, though. You have the patience of a saint."

"I wouldn't go that far." He grabbed my hand and kissed it. "Tell me the truth – do you want children?"

"Yes. I want *your* children. Someday."

Jordan nodded slowly. "We should probably get married first."

I beamed a smile at him. "Is this a wedding proposal?"

His face turned serious. "No. Of course not."

I pretended to pout.

"Look, I'm planning on asking you, eventually. But it's not going to be in a limo or after sex, no matter how amazing it is."

"Let me guess, you're going to make it totally unexpected?"

"Would you expect me to do it any other way?"

"No. I guess not."

"The only problem is, I'm going to have to work harder on fooling you. I still can't believe you made me."

"A woman knows her man," I said, caressing his cheek.

He closed his eyes and hugged me hard. "I don't think I've told you lately, but I fucking love you, Jessica Winters."

"And I fucking love you, too, Jordan Steele."

After a few more kisses, we got dressed and headed back toward the house.

"What were you going to tell me before?" he asked.

I smiled. "'I've invited a few people over for dinner."

He frowned. "It's not just us?"

"No."

He sighed. "I thought it was bad enough that your mother was going to be there."

My jaw dropped. "Jordan... that's not even funny."

"I'm just messing with you," he said, cracking a smile. "I'm sure she's wonderful. I have no doubt, since she's your mother. I'm just not too thrilled with having to sit through dinner with a bunch of strangers."

"You really have to get over your fear of people."

"I'm not afraid of people," he argued. "I just don't care for them too much."

"You're used to being around criminals. Nobody likes them," I said. "The ones you'll be having dinner with are family. Mine and yours."

"Raptor is going to be there?" he asked, staring ahead.

"Yes. So are Adriana and Sammy."

"Who else?"

"Tank. His new girlfriend. Her son, Billy."

"Raina Davis?"

"Yes. Remember I told you that my mother has been watching her boy?"

He nodded.

"So, you see. This won't be so bad."

Jordan mumbled something.

"Hey," I said, grabbing his hand. "If it gets to be too much, we'll go to Plan B."

"What's Plan B?"

"We'll disappear into my bedroom."

He grinned. "And have sex?"

"Of course."

"Can't we just skip to Plan B?"

I laughed. "You won't get any pie if we jump directly to plan B."

He chuckled. "Did you really just say that?"

I slugged him in the arm. "I'm talking *apple* pie."

"I doubt it's as good as yours," he said, a twinkle in his eyes.

"Honey, no matter what happens tonight, I'll make sure you get some pie, one way or another."

"I'll be holding you to it."

"No, I'll be holding *you* to it."

"I love it when you talk fur-pie."

I slugged him.

He laughed.

FORTY FIVE

RAINA

"**B**ILLY, WOULD YOU like to try and say 'Grace'," asked Frannie, as we sat around the dinner table. There were nine of us gathered around. Billy, Sammy, Justin, Raptor, Adriana, Jessica, Jordan, myself, and Frannie.

My son looked around and suddenly became very shy. "No fanks."

Justin and Raptor chuckled.

Frannie gave him a warm smile. "That's okay. What about you, Sammy?"

"I forgot," he said, looking embarrassed.

"I'll help you," said Raptor.

We folded our hands together and Sammy repeated his father's prayer.

"Also, thank you for bringing our family together," added Raptor. "Especially those who are in our hearts even when they aren't always in our lives."

I glanced over at Jessica's boyfriend and noticed his mouth twitch.

"Yes, thank you for bringing Uncle Jordan to us," said Sammy, also sneaking a peek at him. "And we're glad he's safe."

"We're glad all of us are safe," added Raptor. "Amen."

We all said 'Amen' and then we began passing around plates.

"This looks amazing," said Adriana, Raptor's wife. She had dark red hair that was pulled back into a chignon. With her high cheekbones and large eyes, she almost reminded me of Audrey Hepburn.

"Thank you," said Jessica, who, like her mother, had blonde hair and had hazel eyes. "I have to thank my mother for helping, though. Sorry about taking off like that, by the way."

Frannie laughed. "It's okay. You know I enjoy cooking anyway. Besides, Jordan probably wanted some time alone with you before we ambushed him here at the house, right?"

Jordan smiled. "Ambushed," he said, helping himself to the Caesar salad. "Nobody ambushed me."

"So, you knew that we were going to be here the entire time?" asked Raptor, looking amused. "I'm surprised that your limousine didn't suddenly develop a flat tire."

"Actually, he did swerve over to try and hit some glass," said Jessica chuckling.

"Wait a second, you were driving the limo?" asked Justin. "Is that your new gig now? Limo driver?"

"To be honest, I'm not sure what the future holds for me in careers," said Jordan.

"You were a bodyguard before, right?" I asked, a little confused as to where he'd come from and why he was changing careers.

"Yeah. Pretty much," he answered.

Noticing the amusement in his eyes, I asked, "Why the change?"

"Too much traveling involved," he said.

"And it's dangerous," added Jessica. "I don't want him getting shot at."

That made sense.

"If you're looking for a place to work, I can find you a job," said Justin.

"Thanks, but I'm sure I'll figure something out after we get back from Vegas," he replied.

"What about joining the club?" asked Raptor.

"The Gold Vipers?" asked Jordan. "Nah. That's not my gig."

"Besides, that's dangerous, too," said Jessica.

"What's dangerous?" asked Sammy.

"Nothing," said Adriana. "Here, have some vegetables."

He scowled. "I hate asparagus."

"Do you like soup?" asked Billy.

"No," he answered.

"Soup makes you tough," said Billy. "Like Tank."

Justin flexed his muscles. "You know it. So does asparagus, boys."

Sighing, Sammy picked up his fork and stabbed one. He brought it to his lips and took a bite.

"How is it?" asked Raptor.

He shuddered. "I don't like it."

"Sometimes you have to try something a few times before you like it," said Jessica. She looked at Jordan. "In time, it gets easier and much more enjoyable."

Jordan smirked.

"How's your mother, Vanda?" Frannie asked Adriana.

"She's doing well," she replied.

"I'll have to stop by the shop and say 'hi' one of these days."

Listening to the rest of their conversation, I looked around the table and was happy that I'd agreed to have dinner with Justin's friends and family. As time went on, and we uncorked another bottle of wine, even Jordan seemed to relax and open up more.

"I must say, this has been such a lovely time," said Frannie, looking around the table. "And I just know that if Slammer was here, he'd be so proud to have you all at our table."

I stiffened up, suddenly feeling ashamed that I was sitting there.

Noticing my reaction, Justin grabbed my hand under the table. He leaned over and whispered into my ear. "Relax. You're with family. Right where you belong."

I looked around the table and my eyes met with Raptor's.

"She's right," he said, smiling kindly at me. "Slammer would want all of us here, in his house, sharing dinner. Everyone."

Feeling my eyes brim with tears, I looked down and excused myself.

"Where you going?" asked Justin.

"The bathroom. I'll be right back," I said, heading out of the dining room to the bathroom. Inside, I took some time to compose myself and when I felt like I had my shit together, I opened the door.

"Oh. Hey," I said to Justin, who was standing there in the dark hallway.

"You okay?"

I nodded and then noticed that he was holding something behind his back.

"What's going on?"

Smiling, he pulled out a small jewelry box.

"What are you doing?" I asked, a lump suddenly in my throat.

He got down on his knee and looked up at me. "I know that we've just met, but it feels like we've already shared so much together."

I blinked.

"Raina, I don't know how you really feel about me, but I love you. I love you so much that I can't imagine *not* spending the rest of our lives together." He opened up the box and I saw the diamond ring. It sparkled under the light and took my breath away.

"Wait. Stop," I said, tears running down my cheeks. "You know I can't do this. I can't marry you."

"Listen to me," he said, his eyes boring into mine.

"I can't. No," I said waving my hands.

"Raina. For God's sake, listen to me."

I bit my lower lip.

"I'm done with the club."

"What?"

"I've lost my old man. My ex was murdered. My stepsister was attacked. Hell, Adriana was almost killed. I need you in my life but I'm not putting you or Billy in danger again."

I didn't know what to say.

"I refuse to lose you. If I have to give up the club, to be with you, I will, princess."

"But this club is everything to you," I said, remembering the conversation we'd had the other day. The pride and joy in his eyes when he talked about his brothers.

"It is, but you're *more* than everything, if there is such a thing," he said, smiling at me.

"You barely know me."

"I know that I love you. Do you love me?"

"Yes."

"Good. I want to take care of you and Billy. I want to be there for him. I love that kid. You know I do."

"I know you love him, but I can't ask you to quit the club."

"You're not asking me to do anything. I'm telling you what I'm going to do." He grabbed my left hand and placed the ring on my finger.

"I'm stepping down and moving on. Raptor will take over as Prez."

I stared down at the ring. Yes, I loved him. But, I was also frightened. Frightened that he'd regret what he'd done and someday even hate me for it.

I took off the ring and handed it to him. "I'm sorry. I *can't* allow you to do this."

His face fell.

"It's wrong," I said. I touched his face. "I love you. I really do. But... I can't be the reason you leave your club. Not when I know, deep down, it means so much to you."

"So, either way, you're telling me no?"

"Don't make it sound like it's an easy thing," I said, watching his eyes harden.

He dropped the ring into the box and shoved it into his pocket. "I guess there's nothing more to say, then, is there?" he said, not meeting my eyes.

I just stared at him, not sure how to respond. He'd backed me into a corner and now was angry that I wanted what was best for him.

Justin turned around and headed toward the front door.

"Where are you going?"

He turned around on his heel. "You really don't expect me to sit next to you during dinner after being rejected like that, do you?"

"I'm sorry. Maybe I should be the one to go," I said, feeling sick to my stomach.

"No. Billy shouldn't have to leave because of this. Let him finish his dinner."

"Justin," I said as he turned around and continued walking.

"Please... don't walk out like this."

Ignoring me, he stepped out the door and slammed it shut so hard, that the entire house shook.

"What's going on?" asked Frannie, coming up behind me.

"I think I made a terrible mistake," I whispered.

FORTY SIX

TANK

MY HEART FELT like it had been ripped out of my chest and then grated like cheese. Wallowing in self-pity, I got on my bike and drove to Griffin's. When I walked into the bar, Cheeks, who was bartending, waved me over.

"Hi, doll," I said, forcing a smile to my face.

"Hey, I thought you were supposed to be at some dinner engagement right about now?"

"Plans changed," I said. "Give me a bottle of whiskey. Please."

Her eyes widened. "The whole bottle?"

I turned to look at the stripper that was on stage, hoping she be a good distraction. "Yep. Don't ask."

Cheeks brought over a bottle and a shot glass. "Here you go, Tank. Look, if you need someone to talk to, I'm always here for you."

Most of our time talking, in the past, had been in the bedroom and not about any problems, but I could tell she was being sincere. "Thanks, Cheeks. How's business tonight?" It was a Friday night and the place was starting to fill up.

"Decent. Have a new stripper, if you haven't noticed."

I stared at the brunette on stage. She had a huge rack and dark eyes that I decided would look good next to my dick. "Who hired her?"

"She said you did."

I whipped my head around. "Me? I don't think so."

Cheeks laughed. "I'm kidding. I hired her. Thought we could use some new flesh."

I drank down the whiskey and poured myself another shot. "New flesh," I repeated.

"You should go and say 'hi' when she's done with her set. I know she'd love to meet you."

"Maybe I will," I said, kicking back the other one.

"**WHAT'S YOUR NAME**, sweetheart?" I asked the stripper thirty minutes later. We were in my office and she was sitting on the edge of my desk.

"Candace," she said, swinging her leg back and forth.

"Let me guess, they call you Candy?"

"Usually after they get a taste," she said, giggling. "Yes."

I ran my hand over her leg, trying to feel something. Anything. But all I could feel was my anger toward Raina at the moment.

"So, you're the president of the Gold Vipers?" she asked, twirling a strand of hair around her finger.

"Yeah, that's me," I said, sitting back in my chair.

"That's cool," she said, hopping off my desk.

"How old are you?"

"Twenty-one."

I snorted. "Right."

"How old do you want me to be?" she asked, getting on my lap.

"Legal."

She began grinding her crotch against mine, giving me a free lap dance. "I'm barely legal, baby," she whispered in my ear. "Just like you boys like it."

"I'm not like the other boys."

She touched my bulge. "I can tell. You're one of the big boys."

She was soft and sweet in all the right places. I could just tell. But my mind was elsewhere.

"Time to get off the ride, darlin'."

Her eyes widened. "What?"

"I'm not in the mood."

"You feel like you're in the mood."

"That's only half-cocked."

Her eyes widened.

"Go on now. I need to go through some of the accounting." Fortunately, I'd stopped at four shots of whiskey, realizing that I was about to start drunk-texting Raina. There was no way I'd let myself be that much of a pussy.

She stood up and walked around the other side of the desk. "Fine. If you feel up to it later, look me up. I'm on until midnight."

"I'll let you know," I said, turning on the laptop.

"By the way," she leaned over, her cleavage practically in my face. "I can usually suck a guy off in two minutes or less. It's all in the tongue."

My dick twitched. "I'll keep that in mind."

"I'll check on you soon. In case you change it."

"Be my guest," I said, more amused than anything. The girl was damn confident and I hoped it would bring in more customers.

She winked and left my office.

Two minutes later, my attention was on the payables, when someone entered the room. Thinking it Candace, I didn't even look up "My dick isn't ready right now."

"Really?" said a voice dryly.

I looked up to find Raina standing there. She was wearing a long over-coat and had a funny smile on her face.

"What are you doing here?" I asked stiffly.

"You don't look very happy to see me," she said.

I leaned back in the chair. "That's because... I'm not."

"Let me try and change that," she said, opening up the coat. Underneath, she wore nothing but a pair of high heels, black panties, and the cut I'd tried giving her earlier.

My cock jumped to attention.

She walked around the desk and stared down at me. "Well?"

"What's this about?"

She took a deep breath. "I came here to tell you that... I fucked up. Badly."

I wanted nothing more than to bend her over and fuck the hell out of her. But, I kept my cool. "So, what are you saying?"

"That I can't live without you either, Justin." Her eyes filled with tears. "I love you more than... more than anything. I'm sorry about earlier. I was just scared and –"

"Did you really think you could just walk in here, dressed like that, and think everything would be good between us?" I asked.

She looked hurt. "Yeah. I guess so." She pulled the coat around her body. "Apparently, I made another mistake by coming here."

FORTY SEVEN

RAINA

I TURNED TO WALK away when Justin grabbed my arm. He tugged the coat off of me.

"Where in the fuck are you going?" he growled.

Before I could respond, he had me bent over his desk and was standing behind me. I closed my eyes and moaned as his fingers slid under my panties.

"Tell me what you want from me," he demanded, pushing my legs farther apart.

"You," I panted.

"Me? Which part?" I heard him unzip his fly and then felt the tip of his cock circling my opening. "This?"

"Oh, my God, yes," I moaned, wanting him to stick it in.

He pulled away. "My dick, huh? That's it?"

I stiffened up. "No. Of course not."

"So, you want all of me?" he asked.

"Yes."

"You sure about that?"

"Yes."

Justin gripped my hips and I gasped as he plunged into my hole. He pulled out and did it again, this time harder. From this angle, I felt every inch of him, stretching me so wide, it almost hurt.

"I bet you feel me now. All the way to your tonsils." He slid his hands under the cut, running them over my breasts. "My God, you're sexy."

He pinched my right nipple and rolled it between his thumb and index finger. "I know what you want. I know you, Raina. Just like

313

you know me now. Every damn inch of me."

I gripped the edge of the desk, tilting my hips so I could feel every damn inch of his cock.

He pulled out and slid back in. "You want me to fuck you faster, don't you?"

"Yes."

"I want to hear you beg for it," he said, moving his fingers down to my clit. He began rubbing it. "Come on, darlin'."

"Please."

His fingers played me; I couldn't do anything but fall back into the intensity of his touch as he strummed me like a guitar.

"Talk to me."

"Fuck me faster. Please," I moaned.

Justin began thrusting harder and the desk moved as he pumped, but it didn't slow him down.

"You going to come for me?" He put more pressure on my clit, rough and demanding until I screamed out an orgasm.

"Oh, my God," I gasped, as the tremors ran through me.

Trevor stiffened up and grunted in my hair as he came. "I love you," he breathed into my ear huskily.

"I love you, too," I replied, still trying to catch my breath.

A sudden knock made us both jump.

"Hey," said a woman, peeking around the doorway. When she saw us, she didn't even look surprised.

"Cheeks. You need to learn to knock," said Justin, still leaning over me.

She grinned. "I take it this is the one who's gotten you so flustered."

He just sighed.

"Uh, hi. I'm Raina."

"Nice to meet you," she said holding out her hand to shake mine and then quickly lowering it. "Maybe another time."

"What did you need?" asked Justin tersely.

"Just wanted to tell you we need more vodka from downstairs."

"Can't you get it yourself?"

"Hell no. There are rats down there."

"I'll be out in a minute," said Tank.

"Okay. Uh, sorry again," she said, closing the door.

"Well, that was awkward," I said, as Justin pulled out of me. "Although, she seems really nice."

"She is," he said, grabbing some tissues.

I turned around and looked at him. "I really am sorry. I hope you know that."

He stared at me hard. "Sorry enough to marry me?"

I smiled. "If you still want me. And Billy, of course."

He tossed the tissue into the trash can and then pulled me into his arms. "Did you really think that I'd stop loving you in less than two hours? It doesn't work that way."

I lay my cheek against his chest. "I know."

"Are you sure this is what you want?" he asked, rubbing my back.

"I know exactly what I want. You. I'm just a little nervous about what all that entails."

"I told you I'd quit the club if you wanted."

I looked up at him and shook my head. "No. You will always be part of this club. It's in your blood. As long as you can keep us safe, though, I'm willing to try anything."

He tipped my chin up and stared into my eyes. "I'd rather die than let anything happen to either of you."

"I know," I said, seeing the truth in his eyes.

We kissed again and then he handed me my overcoat. "Put this on and we'll get out of here."

"Are you sure? It seems I'm a little overdressed for this place," I said, smiling wickedly. "Besides, I saw a sign near the door that you were hiring dancers. Maybe I should apply."

"Darlin', you can apply all you want, since I'm the owner. But nobody is seeing you naked, but me."

"You do realize that also goes both ways," I said.

"I know."

"And, you're not going to have any club girlfriends or whores." I'd seen quite a bit of things going on during my stay at the club. Not with Justin or Raptor but with a lot of the other members.

"You have nothing to worry about." He pulled the ring back out.

I took the box from him and put the ring back on.

"Do you like it?" he asked. "If you don't we can pick something else out."

"I love it," I replied, holding it out. It was beautiful and bigger than anything I deserved.

"Good, because Billy helped me pick it out."

My jaw dropped. "He knew about this?"

"Of course. I told him I was going to marry his mommy. He was excited and asked if he could call me 'daddy'."

"What did you say?"

"I told him I'd be honored."

"That's sweet. I can't believe that he kept it a secret, though."

"Oh, he wanted to tell you. I had to bribe him in order to keep him from talking."

I smile. "Really? How? With candy?"

"No. A trip to Disney World."

My smile fell. "You promised him a trip to Disney World?"

"Let's just say that we're spending our honeymoon with Mickey Mouse and Ariel."

"Are you okay with that?" I asked, feeling giddy about it myself. I'd never been to Disney World.

"Sure. I guess I've always been dying to find out whether she was a true fire-pelt."

I slugged him. "You're such a perv."

"You're the one who showed up here half-naked," he said, laughing.

"What can I say – you've corrupted me."

"See what you have to look forward to?" he asked, kissing my hand.

"I wouldn't have it any other way," I told him.

"You will have it all kinds of ways when I'm done with you, princess," he said, smiling darkly.

"Promise?"

He slid his hand under my jacket again and touched my ass crack. "Definitely. In fact, I have just the way to consummate that promise."

I sucked in my breath as he slipped his finger in unchartered territory.

"Justin…" I warned.

He sighed and removed his hand. "Fine. Can we at least get some ice cream on the way home?"

When he wasn't thinking of food, he was thinking of sex. *God, I loved this man...*

I smiled. "Yes."

THE END